The Cricket War

For my dad, Bryan — T.P.

For Doug — S.M.

Dedicated to the many Boat People who fled Vietnam from the 1970s to mid-1990s and currently live scattered around the globe, and in memory of those whose remains rest at the bottom of the South China Sea.

This is based on a true story.

Many of the designations used by manufacturers and sellers to distinguish their products are claimed as trademarks. Where those designations appear in this book and Kids Can Press Ltd. was aware of a trademark claim, the designations have been printed in initial capital letters (e.g., Mountain Dew).

Credits
Chapter 8: The legend of Sơn Tinh and Thủy Tinh is adapted from various versions of this legend. Chapter 14: Papa's speech is adapted from Captain Rolf Wangnicks's speech recorded by Norman Aisbett in "Salvation at Sea," *The West Australian*, October 3, 1981. Chapter 18: The legend of the banyan tree was adapted by Thọ from various versions of this traditional Vietnamese tale. Authors' notes: Source for statistics is the *Encyclopedia of Canada's People*, Paul Robert Magocsi, editor, University of Toronto Press, Toronto, 1999.

Published in Canada and the U.S. by Kids Can Press Ltd.

25 Dockside Drive, Toronto, ON M5A 0B5

Kids Can Press is a Corus Entertainment Inc. company

www.kidscanpress.com

The artwork in this book was rendered digitally.
The text is set in Baskerville.

Edited by Patricia Ocampo
Designed by Marie Bartholomew
Cover illustration by Tenzin Tsering

Printed and bound in Canada in 6/2023 by Friesens

CM 23 0 9 8 7 6 5 4 3 2 1

FSC
www.fsc.org
MIX
Paper from
responsible sources
FSC® C016245

Library and Archives Canada Cataloguing in Publication

Title: The cricket war / by Thọ Phạm and Sandra McTavish.
Names: Phạm, Thọ, author. | McTavish, Sandra, author.
Identifiers: Canadiana (print) 20220458103 | Canadiana (ebook) 20220458111 |
ISBN 9781525306556 (hardcover) | ISBN 9781525312052 (EPUB)
Classification: LCC PS8625.T38 C75 2023 | DDC jC813/.6—dc23

Kids Can Press gratefully acknowledges that the land on which our office is located is the traditional territory of many nations, including the Mississaugas of the Credit, the Anishnabeg, the Chippewa, the Haudenosaunee and the Wendat peoples and is now home to many diverse First Nations, Inuit and Métis peoples.

We thank the Government of Ontario, through Ontario Creates, the Ontario Arts Council; the Canada Council for the Arts; and the Government of Canada for supporting our publishing activity.

The Cricket War

by Thọ Phạm and Sandra McTavish

Kids Can Press

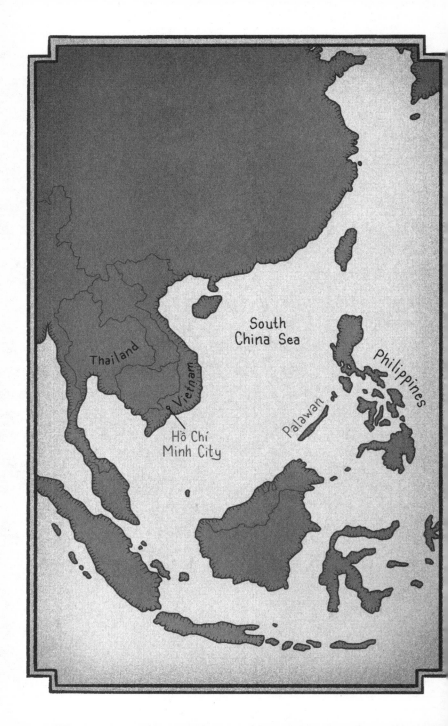

Pronunciation Guide

Name or Word	Who or What	Pronunciation
An	Lâm's older brother	an
ào bà ba	traditional outfit worn in rural Vietnam	OW beh bah
Cuội	a lumberjack in Vietnamese legend	COO-oy
Huấn	the translator on *Cap Anamur*	h-won
Huy	a man from Palawan	wee
Lâm	Thọ's best friend from home	lum
Lan	a teenager from the camp in Manila	lan
Linh	Thọ's aunt	lin
Mai	Lâm's older sister	my
Minh	a thief	min
Mr. Bình	a man who organizes escapes	bin
Mỹ Nương	a princess in Vietnamese legend	MIH NOO-ung
Phát	Thọ's cousin	fat
Quang	Thọ's uncle who lives in America	kwang
Quỳnh	a bully	kwin
Sang	Thọ's neighbor	sang
Sơn Tinh	Lord of the Mountain in Vietnamese legend	sun DHIN
Tâm	Thọ's neighbor	tum
tạt lon	a game	tat lawn
Tết Trung Thu	Lunar New Year	TAYT choong too
Thảo	Thọ's older sister	tow
Thầy Sơn	Thọ's teacher	tey surn
Thọ	a boy from South Vietnam	taw
Thủy Tinh	Lord of the Sea in Vietnamese legend	toy-EE DHIN
Tiên	Thọ's older sister	tee-EN
Việt	Thọ's friend from *Cap Anamur*	vee-ET
Vũ	Thọ's older brother	voo
xe lam	a three-wheeled vehicle	sair lam

A note on usage: Vietnamese kids use "mother" and "father" and are always consistent in that form. This is why words like "mom" and "dad" aren't used in this book. Similarly, Vietnamese say "America" not the "United States." The word "anh" is a respectful way of addressing someone. It technically means "brother."

CHAPTER 1

Hồ Chí Minh City (formerly Sài Gòn)

April 1980

"Mine's going to bite the leg off yours, Thọ." Lâm smiles devilishly, rubbing his hands with glee.

"That's what you said before the last fight," I laugh, not at all fazed by the threat. "And remember how it turned out?"

Lâm rolls his eyes. The last fight had not gone his way.

I add, "I believe I've won the last four fights. No … the last five fights. That'll make this one number six."

"*If* you win," interrupts Lâm.

"*When* I win."

"Okay, Thọ, let's get started."

We are sitting in the doorway of my house. We've each chosen a cricket for the duel. Lâm, who lives next door, has brought his insect in a matchbox, which he carefully holds in the palms of his hands. His black cricket chirps and nibbles on a piece of banana Lâm has given him, unaware that he's about to go into battle.

All the boys we know like cricket fighting. But Lâm takes it more seriously than most. Although he spends more time training his crickets than I do, they rarely win. That's why he doesn't have nearly as many as I have.

I use a cardboard box to make a housing complex for my crickets. I separate the insects in walled, cardboard compartments with a screen covering the top of the box, so they can get air but won't escape. I feed them pieces of banana, lettuce and grass, and train them to act aggressively by taunting them with a dead cricket's head mounted on the end of a toothpick.

Lâm and I have always lived next door to each other. We're both eleven years old and have been best friends for as long as I can remember. We're opposites, and that's why we get along so well. I'm the shortest in the class, and he's the tallest. Lâm is a jokester who doesn't pay attention in school. The only things he's serious about are cricket fighting, which he never wins, and soccer, which he's amazing at. I am quieter and do well in school and some of the things my mother wishes that I didn't do well in, like cricket fighting. Each day after school, we either play soccer or fight crickets. Lâm doesn't usually complain when his crickets lose to mine, and I never grumble when he scores on me in soccer.

With cricket fighting, the rules never change. The winner gains the loser's cricket. And if the losing cricket dies in battle (as sometimes happens), the loser gives the winner another of his crickets.

Resting between Lâm and me sits a small box in which the war will take place.

I examine my crickets and select my prized fighter from my collection and put him in the small box. Then Lâm carefully takes his cricket out of his matchbox. While he takes his time placing it in the box next to mine, I pluck a hair out of my head that I plan to dangle in front of the insects, tickling them in an attempt to aggravate them and make them want to fight. Instead of using the hair to provoke the crickets, I reach over and tickle Lâm's cheek. This startles him, and he drops his cricket into the box.

"Hey!" But he doesn't have time to get mad as the two crickets puff their wings and chirp frantically. Then Lâm's hops toward mine and bites him. Mine bites right back — harder and more vicious. Bite. Bite. Chirp. Chirp. The insects lock their bodies in a feisty embrace. Suddenly, thirty seconds into the fight, Lâm's cricket flees from my champion and seeks protection in a corner of the box. My cricket flutters his wings and chirps a victorious cry.

"Yes!" I punch my fists into the air. "What did I tell you? That's six in a row." I quickly retrieve the crickets, placing them one at a time in separate stalls in my cardboard complex, rewarding each of them with a piece of lettuce.

"You cheated!" Lâm whines. "My cricket wasn't ready when I dropped him into the box." Lâm looks disappointed as he picks up his empty matchbox. "I'm running out of crickets. I'm going to have to buy some more at this rate."

"I'm running out of room in my cardboard box. I'm going to have to make another box at this rate," I tease.

Lâm gives me a friendly slug. "I'd better head home, Thọ. My mother will have dinner ready."

"Mine, too. Do you want to have another cricket battle on Monday?"

"Let's play soccer instead. I need to stock up and train some crickets before we have another battle."

"I could always sell you one of my crickets. I've got so many," I joke as I pick up my cardboard box. "Have a good weekend," I add before entering my house.

My front door opens into a living room, with only a three-seater couch and a matching chair. My brother Vũ and two sisters Thảo and Tiên are sitting on the couch, talking about typical teenager things that don't interest me. They ignore me as I crouch down and place my box of crickets in the corner. My mother will make me move it at bedtime because the sound of the crickets chirping drives her crazy when she tries to sleep. As I stand up, Vũ looks over at me.

"How'd you do?" Vũ asks.

"I won!"

"That's great. That's five in a row, isn't it?"

"No, it's six," I boast.

"Since you keep winning, Lâm must almost be out of crickets."

"He's definitely getting low. I told him he could buy some from me if he wanted." We both laugh.

Stretched along the far wall is a narrow staircase

leading up to a small room that I have only visited a handful of times. This is my father's room. My mother calls it his escape and lets us kids know that we're not allowed up there under any condition without his permission. The first time my father invited me to his room, I was so excited! I thought it had treasures or gold or something special. But I was completely disappointed — the room only has a desk and chair, a radio, some books and a sleeping mat for my father.

I leave my siblings in the living room and walk into the dining room. Our dining room used to have a table and chairs. After the Communists captured Sài Gòn, and all of South Vietnam, in the spring of 1975, my father lost his well-paying job at the bank. Although my mother didn't work beforehand, after that she and my father both got jobs. But they didn't make nearly enough. To make ends meet, they started selling household items, including the dining room furniture. Now the room remains empty. At night, the dining room transforms into a bedroom where I sleep beside my mother, my brother and two sisters on mats on the cool, ceramic floor.

Past the dining room is a tiny, open courtyard. On one side of the courtyard is the washroom. A large tank on top of the washroom collects rainwater from the roof. If there hasn't been any rain for a while, we get water from our neighbor's well and carry it home in buckets, one bucket in each hand.

Beyond the washroom is the kitchen. Delicious smells drift from the clay stove in the kitchen where my mother has been cooking dinner. "You're almost late," she says, handing me a pair of chopsticks and a bowl of rice and pork chops with lemongrass. I bow my head and sheepishly join her with the rest of the family to eat.

After dinner, I sit on the couch to work on my math homework. I tap my pencil against my notebook while trying to solve a problem.

"I remember learning this," Vũ says. I jump and then sigh. I hadn't noticed him standing over me. "The square of the hypotenuse is equal to the sum of the squares on the other two sides." I give him a puzzled look. "Here, I'll show you the formula to solve it." He sits beside me, takes the notebook and pencil and gives me a mini math lesson.

"Thanks," I say.

"No problem. It's easy if you stop to think about it," Vũ teases, ruffling my hair. I shake my head quickly to get my hair back in place. Vũ is right. I usually learn quickly — when I pay attention.

***

On Monday morning, as is the case every morning, church bells wake me. I lie in bed with my eyes closed and listen to them for a minute before I get up. I don't want to rise yet. I sleep next to Vũ, who often battles nightmares. His tossing and turning woke me in the night.

I drag myself out of bed, roll up my sleeping mat,

fold my blanket, wash, put on my school uniform — navy pants and a white shirt — eat my breakfast of steamed yam, and go out to meet Lâm. Every school morning, Lâm meets me on the street outside my front door.

As I wait for my best friend, the fat yellow sun pokes above the gray houses. Its warm rays cast a long shadow over the rooftops, creating a perfect shade for me. At least it's still the dry season — for a few more weeks — so I don't need to worry about standing in the rain. Friends and neighbors walk past, and we say hello. A couple of stray dogs stroll by, sniffing the ground and ignoring me. Down the street, a cat meows. The dogs jerk their heads up. Then they start barking and chase the cat. Tâm's baby is crying again. On quiet nights, I can hear his wails through our common wall. My neighbor Sang's pigs make lots of noise when they are hungry. Their grunts are so loud that I know they haven't been fed yet.

After ten minutes, I am tired of waiting. I call Lâm's name, knowing he can hear me from inside his house. He doesn't answer. The door is shut. I knock. Again, no answer. Lâm's home is smaller than mine, so I know someone inside could hear me if anyone was home. Lâm is usually the last person to leave in the morning. His parents go to work early and his older brother, An, and sister, Mai, start school before us. It's not unusual that they're not home. But it's strange that Lâm isn't here. He would normally tell me if he couldn't walk to school with me. Perhaps Lâm wanted help with his homework so he could pass the math test tomorrow, and left early. I don't have time to wander around the neighborhood looking for him. If I don't get to school soon, I'll be late.

***

I walk down my street, which is just wide enough for one car. I stroll past door after door of house after house. The front of each house faces the narrow roadway and hugs the house on either side, allowing no space between the buildings. Each front door opens right into the street. I feel as if the windows and doors are eyes watching me. Since I've lived on this street my entire life, each house is like an old, familiar friend. I know the families in every home. Neighbors see each other pass by every day. No one is a stranger, and no one feels alone.

My street eventually joins a slightly wider and more crowded one. It is filled with people riding bicycles; others are walking and some zip along on scooters. The smell of vehicle exhaust and cooking mixes in the air. I pass a row of homes where people sell food and other items from their front rooms. Small shops with wide doorways open to the street outside.

Then I walk by my favorite street vendor who is always cooking roast pork. I take a deep breath, allowing the scent of the meat to float down into my stomach.

As I walk to school, I keep an eye out for Lâm. But there is no sign of him.

In the schoolyard, the kids gather in small groups of either boys or girls. No Lâm. He's probably inside getting extra help. He always tries to get higher marks than me in school, but it rarely happens.

The bell rings. I enter the classroom. Thầy Sơn starts the lesson, and still no Lâm. My stomach clenches, but I try to ignore it and imagine there is a good reason Lâm isn't at home or school and didn't tell me, his best friend, about his plans.

After school, I want to knock on Lâm's door and ask where he is. But everything is so strange I decide to act normal. I should pretend that I haven't realized Lâm has been away from school all day.

I join a few of the neighborhood boys for a game of soccer in the street. No one seems fazed when Lâm doesn't join us, even though he has never missed an after-school soccer game before. In the last five years, people from the neighborhood have disappeared at random times. We all know about it, but no one says anything. So it's not surprising when no one mentions Lâm. But my stomach squeezes so tightly I can hardly breathe.

Just before the game begins, a voice calls out from Lâm's doorway: "Can I play?" The voice belongs to Lâm's sister, Mai, who is two years older than Lâm and me. We eagerly agree.

"They need a player." I nod toward the other team, who has one less person. Mai walks right over to them, stands in front of the flip-flops we use for goalposts and faces me and my team. Most Vietnamese girls don't play soccer — in fact, they rarely play with boys at all — but Mai isn't like most Vietnamese girls. She plays soccer better than most of us.

I like Mai. Her long, shiny hair runs down her back, and her eyes sparkle the way raindrops glisten on banana tree leaves. I also like that she always says "hello" and doesn't ignore me the way some of my friends' older sisters do.

I want to ask Mai about Lâm, but before I get a chance, the soccer game begins. No matter how hard we try, Mai jumps and dives and stops the ball.

"Hey, Mai! Look at this!" I call out to her during the game. I make a face with my eyes, rolling them back in my head, and I stick my tongue out sideways, hoping this will distract Mai. She doesn't laugh. She doesn't even blink. Two seconds later, she stops a hard shot from one of my friends that I couldn't have stopped in my dreams. My team loses the game, failing to score a single goal.

After the game, everyone heads home. Before Mai disappears into her house, I seize my chance and ask her: "Is Lâm okay? He wasn't at school today."

"Yes, he's fine," she says quickly. "My uncle in the country is very sick, so Lâm and An went to help with his farm." Although Mai looks me right in the eye, and although she doesn't hesitate in her response, I know she isn't telling the truth. Lâm would never leave without saying goodbye.

My heart sinks to the hot pavement. Since the Communists took over five years ago, many people have escaped. I think of all the friends and neighbors who just disappeared, one by one, two by two or — if they could afford it or were lucky — as a family. But most often it was like this. A son would be sent away so he wouldn't be conscripted into the Communist army. The Communists have taken away our freedom. Boys have to fight for them, farmers must give them their land, people must give them their possessions. And if anyone refuses, the Communists force them to do what they want. They try to control what we learn, and what we know.

When Mai tells me Lâm is gone and has left without saying goodbye, I know my best friend and his older brother are gone from our neighborhood for good. I also know that I must pretend that Lâm is at his uncle's house and not ask any more questions. And I also know Mai will never tell me the truth. She can't risk telling me where Lâm and An are because if the Communists discover they have fled from Vietnam, they will find ways to make Mai and her parents' lives miserable.

Mai stands in front of her house; I stand in front of mine. We stare at each other, not saying a word. Not moving. And not expressing any emotions. I try to think of something to say, but I only have questions about Lâm, and I know Mai wouldn't — or shouldn't — answer them.

"Good game," I finally blurt out, breaking the

silence. A lump in my throat makes my voice crack a little. "You're a great goalie."

"Thanks."

We remain where we are, so quiet that I can hear Mai's breathing. We look into each other's eyes for a second, and then cast our eyes down to the ground. The setting sun drags our long, dark shadows across the street.

Eventually, I raise my right hand and give Mai a gentle wave.

"See you later, Mai."

"See you later, Thọ."

Then Mai walks into her house, and I walk into mine as if this is an ordinary day. As if my best friend in the whole world hasn't disappeared. As if the Communists don't exist. As if our country isn't divided between two groups — the Communists and the rest of us.

As soon as I step inside, I take a long, deep breath and cry on the inside but not the outside.

I know why Lâm has left. And I accept it. It is how it has been for years now. But I don't know where he's gone or if I will ever see him again. I am scared for him and his brother and what might be happening to them. But I am also scared for Mai and their parents. If the Communists figure out that Lâm and An are not with their uncle, I don't know if I can accept what will happen.

CHAPTER 2

Hồ Chí Minh City

April 1980

As I walk up my street after school the next day, I see two soldiers banging on Lâm's front door. One of them barks Lâm's brother's name and orders, "Come outside right now."

No one answers the door. Lâm's parents would still be at work, and if Mai is home from school, she's pretending that she's not there.

Instead of scurrying into my house, I walk up to the soldiers and ask boldly, "Are you looking for An?" I have no idea why I am doing this. My mouth goes dry, and I lick my lips. The soldiers stop pounding on the door and look at me with disgust.

"Of course we're looking for him," one soldier snaps. "Why do you think I just shouted his name?"

"Well, you won't find him here," I say. "He's gone." Now that I've got their attention, I realize I need to make something up quickly. The soldiers won't believe the lie Mai told me yesterday. Even if they do believe the story of An visiting a sick uncle, they would likely punish Mai and her parents for not sending An to the army instead. They would have no sympathy for sick relatives. "Some soldiers came yesterday and took him away." I look them right in the eye just like Mai did when she lied to me and hope they can't tell how scared I am.

"Are you sure?" one soldier asks.

"Yes, I saw them."

The soldiers look at each other and shrug their shoulders. "There must be some mistake." They get onto their motorcycles and drive down the street.

Instead of entering my house, I keep walking down the street in case the soldiers are looking. I do not want them to know where I live, especially when they discover An isn't in the army. I try to appear as if nothing weird has just happened, and as if I didn't just lie to Communist soldiers. My breathing doesn't slow until I am at the end of my street.

After wandering around the neighborhood for ten minutes, I feel safe enough to go home. As I step in the living room, Vũ pounces on me. "I heard you with the soldiers, Thọ. You shouldn't have lied to them."

"I know. But if I didn't lie and they discover An is gone, they'd punish Mai and her parents."

"They could punish you if they figure out you didn't tell the truth."

"They'll never remember my face, and they don't know where I live. They'll never find me."

"Well, they'll find me soon," Vũ says. I look at my brother. He's also one of the shortest kids in his class and could easily pass as younger except for the shadow of a mustache that darkens every few weeks. But it doesn't matter what he looks like. The government knows he is almost eighteen, just a few months younger than An. My brother has a look of fear in his eyes that I've never seen before.

"We need to do something to make sure that doesn't happen," I say.

Vũ rubs his face with both of his hands. His head snaps up. "My friend's brother cut off his trigger finger so the army wouldn't want him."

I immediately insist, "You should do that, too." The faces of those soldiers fill my mind.

"Let's find a sharp knife and do it right now. Before I change my mind."

Vũ and I look for a sharp knife and some rags to soak up the blood. We find what we need in a matter of minutes.

"Now what?" Vũ asks me as if I've cut off a finger before.

"Let's do it in the courtyard. It will be easier to clean up the blood there."

"You'll have to cut it for me, Thọ. I can't do it myself."

My stomach tightens. I feel nauseated. I had assumed Vũ would cut off his own finger. I need to appear brave in front of my older brother, but I really don't want to chop his finger off.

We go to the courtyard and put some rags on the

ground. Then we crouch down. Vũ holds out his hand, and I take the knife. He curls in his other fingers, so only the trigger finger is extended. I raise the knife in the air, staring at my brother's finger, wondering what it will feel like to cut through skin and bone.

I hear my father shout, "What's going on?"

I drop the knife onto the ground and look at Vũ, whose face has turned white. I explain everything to my father. The soldiers at Lâm's door looking for An. My lie. Vũ's fear of being conscripted. The plan to cut off his finger.

"You boys are crazy," my father snaps. "A missing finger isn't going to stop you from getting conscripted, Vũ. That act of defiance will only encourage them. Now put that knife and those rags away, and stop being foolish."

My father marches back to his room while Vũ and I put everything away. I wander back out to the courtyard alone and look down, spreading my fingers apart, wondering what it would feel like to lose one. If my father hadn't interrupted us, Vũ would now have a bloody stub instead of a tenth finger.

Vũ and I don't say anything about it for the rest of the evening, but I know we are thinking the same thing: it's only a matter of time before they come after him, too.

CHAPTER 3

Hồ Chí Minh City

May 1980

In the weeks after Lâm disappeared and I almost cut off Vũ's finger, my parents whisper like snakes hissing. I try to decode their whispers but they somehow always know when I am listening. They change the subject or end their conversation before I can figure out what they are saying. Then one day, while dressing for school, my father says to Vũ and me, "You won't need to wear your uniform today. You're not going to school. Come up to my room and I'll explain."

I am confused but don't ask any questions. I obediently put on my shorts and T-shirt — the only clothes I have apart from my uniform — and climb the stairs to my father's room. My father sits at his desk while Vũ and I stand respectfully. My eyes quickly dart around the room. In the handful of times I've been in this room, it always looks the same. The only furniture is a desk and chair. The radio is still there, as is a bunch of books. I look up at Vũ and widen my eyes slightly. *Do you know what this is about?* As if he could read my mind, my brother responds by shaking his head.

My father clears his throat and says, "For a thousand years, Vietnam was under Chinese rule. Then for another hundred years, we were under French rule. After centuries of being led by other countries, we wanted to rule ourselves and become independent. We were finally free from foreign control when the Communists defeated the French in 1954. After that, we were divided into two almost even halves: North Vietnam and South Vietnam, with the Communists controlling the north.

"That year a lot of people migrated to the south, including your mother's family and me. We settled in this city so we didn't have to live under Communist regime."

I've heard this story so many times that I want to roll my eyes and sarcastically say, "Yes, I know this story. You've told it to me a million times before." But of course I don't say that and neither does Vũ. We simply nod.

"For many years, the Americans tried to help prevent the spread of Communism from the north to the south, but even they couldn't succeed."

Even though I was only six years old when the last American troops left our city, I still remember the day. I was in the living room, and my father startled me when he entered the house. He was home much earlier than usual. My mother rushed into the room to greet him and ask him if he was okay. My father walked over to her and did something he never did in front of us kids — he hugged her. "I could have left Vietnam today," he explained, "through work. But I couldn't do it. I couldn't leave you all behind." Then my mother did something unexpected — she kissed him.

I look at my father as he continues, "My worst nightmares came true as the north took over the south and forced us to be under Communist rule."

My father pauses. I know exactly what he's going to say next. I try not to look bored, knowing my father could ramble on for hours about this topic.

"It is torture living in a Communist country," he says angrily. "If you had money, or a big house, or lots of land before the Communist regime, they took it from you. They control what you learn, what you say in public, even how you practice your religion. If you vocally disagree with them, they will silence you by force or intimidation, or send you away to what they call a 're-education' camp. At these camps, people are treated like prisoners and forced to do hard labor. Sometimes they die from starvation or beatings. If you try to leave the country and are caught, you are sent to prison. You also might be tortured or simply disappear."

I shudder slightly and think briefly of Lâm. Many of the people who try to escape don't succeed. Lâm and his brother could be in a prison right now.

My father rises from his chair and looks me directly in the eyes and then turns to Vũ. "As long as I am alive, my sons will not be forced to fight for the Communists. So, I have arranged for you both to leave Vietnam today on a boat owned by someone I know. He's promised to take you to a safe country. Maybe things will change in a few years and you can come back home.

"Vũ, you go and hail a xe lam. We need to leave for his house right away."

I stand still in shock. This is not how I thought my father's speech would go. I thought he was just giving us another history lesson. Not sending us away! I want to scream. I want to cry. And I also won't get to say goodbye to my friends. I want to ask a hundred questions, and beg my father to let me stay or at least consider it. Instead, I stare silently at the floor. We know better than to question our father.

Vũ looks as surprised by this news as I am, though he also doesn't ask any questions. Without saying a word, Vũ hurries down the stairs and outside onto the street to hail a xe lam.

My mother enters the room and hands me a plastic bag. "For your journey," she says. I peer inside and notice an extra pair of shorts, an extra T-shirt and a bag of dehydrated cooked rice. I look at my mother. Her eyes are swollen and red. She wraps her arms around me and holds me for a few minutes in a warm embrace. I stiffen, becoming a stone statue with my arms at my side, not sure how to react to this rare hug.

I feel as if I am in a dream. My parents and I walk down the stairs to the living room where Thảo and Tiên are standing with Vũ, having returned after hiring a xe lam driver. Vũ and I give a nod to our sisters as if we are going to school and will be back in a few hours. Thảo, and Tiên stare at us silently, their eyes wide and lips pressed together tightly. My mother hands Vũ a bag and gives him a hug, too, as her eyes well up with tears.

Then my father, Vũ and I leave the house and climb onto the xe lam. In the street, there are no tearful good-byes. No waving. No staring longingly at the house to make the memory last. We act as if this is an ordinary day, as if I am not leaving my home and maybe my country. I have no idea when I will see my mother and sisters again. How could our goodbye be so quick? How could that be it?

I don't remember any part of the journey. My mind feels as frozen as my body. I don't see the bicycles and motorcycles zipping through the streets, or the merchants selling goods at their roadside stands.

The journey takes five minutes or fifty-five. Time has stopped for me. In what feels like the time it takes to snap my fingers, Vũ and I have gone from our home to the front room of this strange man's house, where we sit silently on a bench in front of a large picture of bright flowers hanging on the wall. Meanwhile, the older man and our father sit in two wooden chairs on the other side of the sparse room. On the coffee table between them sits a teapot and a set of cups.

"Would you like some tea?" the man asks my father.

My father nods. "Thank you, anh Bình," he says as Mr. Bình pours my father a cup and then himself one. The two men pick up their cups and sip their tea in silence for a few minutes. They act as if Vũ and I aren't there.

"You only paid seventy-five grams of gold," states Mr. Bình.

"That is correct," agrees our father.

"Well, that's only enough for one of your sons."

"But that's all the gold I have," pleads our father. He grips his empty cup of tea.

"Surely you have more stashed away somewhere."

"No, I don't. This is everything I've got. It's all my savings."

"Unfortunately, all your savings isn't enough for two boys. I can only take one of them." Mr. Bình takes a sip of his tea, never taking his eyes off my father.

"Please! I beg of you. Take both my sons. You know what the Communists will do to them if they stay. The army uses the South Vietnamese boys on the front lines as targets for the enemy. I couldn't live with that. Please!"

"I can't drop the fee just for you," Mr. Bình explains angrily. "Otherwise, it wouldn't be fair to the others who have paid full price."

My father shakily puts his cup down on the table and folds his hands as if in prayer. "I'll do anything you want. Please take them both."

Mr. Bình bangs his cup down on the table, causing me to jump in my seat. "Look, I don't need to take either of them. You knew the price. A deal is a deal. So, for seventy-five grams, I'll take one boy only."

My father sighs.

Mr. Binh adds, "If you find at least three other

people to pay full price, then I'll lower the price for the second."

"There's no time for that," my father mutters. He turns and briefly looks at us. He scrunches his eyebrows and lowers his eyes. "Vũ is older and will soon be conscripted. Take him. Thọ will stay behind."

I still can't wake up from this bad dream. And in this dreamlike state, for the first time in my life, I hug my brother, and so does my father. Vũ doesn't look at either of us. Pools of tears fill our eyes, ready to tumble down our cheeks at any moment, though somehow they don't. Vũ doesn't make a sound as he slowly stands, holding on tightly to his plastic bag. My heart feels like the plastic bag — the air crushed out of it. I wonder if my brother feels the same.

It was frightening when I thought the two of us would be sent out into the world without our parents. How could Vũ do this on his own? We have never been anywhere outside of Vietnam, and only leave the city to visit my aunt in the countryside. Will Vũ be okay outside Vietnam in the unknown?

Mr. Bình assures our father that my brother will be safe.

I take one last look at my brother, photographing him in my mind. Before I can say more than a few words, Mr. Bình ushers my father and me out onto the street, leaving Vũ behind.

There we hail a xe lam and it meanders slowly through the bustling streets, taking us to our home, which only a few hours before I thought I was leaving for good. Both my father and I look straight ahead during the journey, and we don't say a word to each other.

By the time we return to our house, Thảo and Tiên have already left for school. When we enter the front door, I follow behind my father. Seeing me, my mother's eyes get big and as round as the sun, and she asks, "What happened? Why are you here?" She brushes the back of her hand across her moist eyes. Before I can answer, she squeezes me tight. While my father explains what happened, I slip out of her grasp and crouch beside my cricket box. I stare intensely at my insects. Beneath the screen, each one creeps around its own compartment, fluttering its wings and chirping softly, unaware of anything outside its box.

***

That night, I bury my face into my pillow to muffle my tears. I hardly sleep. An ache in the pit of my stomach keeps me awake. Vũ had been beside me my whole life. I miss him sleeping next to me, hearing him toss and turn with nightmares. We are in a nightmare now.

Lâm is gone. Vũ is gone.

I dream that I am marching away from home, a soldier in the army. For the first time in my life, I don't look forward to the ringing of the church bells waking me up in the morning, reminding me that it's a new day.

CHAPTER 4

Hồ Chí Minh City

May 1981

The days melt into weeks and the weeks into months until a year has passed since the day at Mr. Bình's house. I regularly think about Vũ and Lâm. My heart feels a little emptier with them gone.

A month after Vũ left, my family received a telegram. All it read was *Arrived safely in Malaysia*. Even though it wasn't signed, we knew it was from Vũ. He couldn't sign it and give himself away to the Communists. From this, my family assumes that my brother has made it safely to a refugee camp in Malaysia. A few letters follow the telegram.

Not much has changed for me during the past twelve months except I am a year older and a grade higher in school. Unfortunately, I am not any taller and look the same at age twelve as I did at eleven.

With Lâm gone, the neighborhood soccer ball doesn't get much of a workout. None of us feels like playing anymore. Through hushed chatter with friends and overhearing conversations between adults, I know that many people continue trying to escape from Vietnam.

I still keep some crickets in my cardboard box. My crickets fight other friends' crickets occasionally, though no one humors me with regular fights the way Lâm did. I am still quiet in school and get good marks. But I failed one math test and forgot to finish my homework twice. Neither of those things had ever happened before.

I wonder where Lâm is. I wonder if he has crickets or a new best friend. I know Mai won't tell me anything other than the lie about Lâm and An visiting their uncle's farm. Mai rarely makes eye contact when passing me on the street and no longer speaks a word to me.

In the past year, my house has become emptier. Of course, it feels empty without Vũ. But it is actually emptier — furniture keeps disappearing.

At first, my father sells his desk and chair, and then my mother sells the living room furniture, even the ceiling fan. I know without having to ask that my parents are selling the furniture to earn money for my voyage out of Vietnam.

On the last Saturday in May, my mother shakes me awake and says, "Mr. Bình has disappeared. No one has heard from him in a while."

"Oh." I yawn, wondering why my mother would wake me up to tell me this.

"This morning we're going to Aunt Linh's house." Then my mother hands me a plastic bag. Inside is a spare pair of shorts and a T-shirt. "I sewed a small gold chain into the hem of the shirt," my mother explains. "I've also written the address of Uncle Quang inside it," my mother adds. As she continues, I pull the shirt out of the bag and find an address in America. "Make sure you contact him. He'll help you. There's also some rice. Don't forget to send ... to send ..."

My mother abruptly leaves the room. Her eyes are brimming with tears. This is the moment I realize the trip to my aunt's house is more than a typical visit.

Later that morning, my father hugs me for the first time. The hug is warm but brief. It doesn't feel like a "goodbye — I don't know when or if we'll ever see you again" hug.

I want to cling to my father for hours and beg him to let me stay. My salty tears want to spill from my eyes. But I don't beg or cry. I know that reaction won't help the situation. Neither will it change the inevitable. It will only make the goodbye worse for all of us.

I say, "See you later," to Thảo and Tiên, but I don't hug them. I want to believe I'll be home soon, like last time. Something will prevent the trip from happening. Maybe someone will tip the Communists off and they'll seize the boat.

My mother and I leave the house, taking a xe lam to the bus station. We pretend we're visiting her sister in the countryside for a few nights. The truth is we *are* taking the bus to visit her sister, only I'm not returning home with my mother.

Aunt Linh had told my parents about a boat leaving near her village. They think taking it will be the safest plan for me. The only problem is that my aunt lives in a small village over two hundred kilometers away. With two ferries to cross two different rivers and a bus ride across narrow, bumpy country roads, it takes over ten hours to get to my aunt's.

My mother and I are lucky to get seats on the bus. It's so full even the aisle is crammed with people sitting on their belongings. The bus winds through the overcrowded city past stores, churches and houses, eventually making its way to the country. Mango and other trees grow on either side of the road, their leaves waving at the bus.

After a while, I stop staring out the bus window at the trees and roadside stalls where people sell food and drinks. I think about all the friends I just left behind. I *know* I will see them in a few days. I *will* be back home soon, maybe before the end of the week.

I think of my older brother. He did not get to go back home. His nightmare began that day. I shift in my seat, suddenly feeling cramped. One by one, my friends' faces flash in my mind. Then I think about my crickets. I worry about what might happen to them since neither of my sisters will have anything to do with cricket fighting. I wish I could have given the crickets to one of my friends at school. But doing that might have tipped someone off that I was leaving. I picture my house and Lâm's and all the other houses up and down my street. I also picture waking up in the morning, the sound of the bells in the distance. I picture my walk to school, and the smell of roast pork cooking. I must remember everything.

After a few hours, the bus comes to a river and stops. We pile out, relieved to stretch our legs and take a breath of fresh air. From a roadside stand, my mother buys a coconut to share with me. We join the other bus passengers and walk onto the ferry that will take us across the river. Once the people are aboard, our bus and some other vehicles drive onto the ferry. My mother and I find room on a wooden bench near the back. I poke a hole through the huskless coconut and sip the coconut water through a straw while I try not to breathe in the ferry's engine fumes. My mother has not spoken much the entire trip. I do not feel like speaking either. I worry I might cry, and I do not want people to ask questions.

The ferry chugs slowly to the other side of the river. It reaches land, and the calm from the river ride vanishes. Passengers on foot and in cars all try to leave the ferry at the same time. We make our way back on the bus.

We ride for a few more hours before coming to another river. My whole body hurts from sitting so long. As we climb off the bus, I yawn. I feel like we'll never get to my aunt's. We board a ferry, following the same routine as we did on the first one.

Before climbing back on the bus, my mother instructs the driver where to let us off. An hour later, the bus stops directly in front of my Aunt Linh's place. My aunt sits on a chair on her front veranda, fanning herself, waiting for us. Her light blue ao bà ba hangs down past her waist and matches her baggy pants. Even though she's more than ten years older than my mother, her long black hair makes her look almost the same age. As we exit the bus, she gets up from her chair and waves at us with her fan.

"Thọ, you've grown so much since I last saw you! You're almost a young man now," my aunt greets me. I haven't grown at all since she saw me last year. Still, I appreciate the compliment.

My aunt ushers us inside her home, where she has already prepared dinner for us. As I eat some rice, fried fish, and bitter melon soup — one of my favorites — I can't help thinking that this could be one of the last days I'll spend with my mother. Every hour brings me closer to the moment I have to leave her and Vietnam, and toward a journey I try not to think about.

CHAPTER 5

Tân Hiệp

May 1981

Aunt Linh lives in a quiet village along a river. The front of her blue wooden house faces the street, while the back perches on the water. Her house is quieter and emptier than when I last visited with my mother and sister to celebrate Tết Trung Thu. During that visit, the house was full of laughter and people. Since then, my uncle and their five oldest children have all escaped, leaving my aunt and her youngest son, Phát, all alone in their large house. Phát is two years older than I am and much taller. He regularly reminds me that he's older and taller, and I regularly remind him that I'm faster and smarter, which I'm not sure is true. But it's all I can think of when he teases me.

I wonder if Aunt Linh and Phát will join the rest of their family and escape from Vietnam, but I don't ask any questions about their plans. I don't even ask any questions about my own journey, and no one offers me any details.

Over the next few days, Phát shows me how he takes clay from the riverbanks behind their house and rolls it in his hands, pretending to make hot peppers. We also climb mango trees and construct boats out of banana leaves. Using old plastic bags and thin strips of bamboo, we make kites. Since we don't have tape or glue, we use cooked sticky rice to hold the plastic to the bamboo frame. Then we tie a string to our handmade kites and run up and down the road, trying to make them fly.

"May I borrow one of your flip-flops?" I ask Phát, before we head outside to play tạt lon.

"Why do you want mine? Why not use one of your own?"

"Because mine are too flimsy. I'll have a better chance of winning with yours."

Phát laughs as he hands me one of his firm flip-flops. Then we join two other boys who live nearby in a small clearing. Phát offers to be the "keeper" first. With a stick, he draws a circle in the dirt and places an empty tin can in the middle of the circle. The rest of us line up about ten big steps away. I hold on to my cousin's flip-flop. The other boys kick off their flip-flops and each hold on to one. Then one at a time, we throw our flip-flops at the can, trying to knock it down and make it roll away as far as possible. The two boys throw first, miss the can, and run over to stand next to their flip-flops.

Now it's my turn. I look at Phát, and he grins at me. The other two boys had thrown their flip-flops in a hard downward arc. If they had hit the can, it would have rolled far. But they missed. I take a deep breath, as the other boys cheer me on.

"You can do it, Thọ!"

"Come on!"

I stick my arm out at my hip and whip my flip-flop sideways. It hits the can and clatters out of the circle! I race toward my flip-flop, but Phát is racing toward the can just beyond it. I can hear the two boys yelling. Before I am near my flip-flop, they have grabbed theirs and scurried back to the line. It's just me left! Phát is two paces ahead, and he grabs the can and pivots, almost crashing into me. "Hey!" I crouch down, swipe up my flip-flop, and race back to the line. I see Phát reach the circle, where he slams the can down in the middle of the circle again. Then he bounces back up, and I swerve to avoid him, but he reaches out a surprisingly long arm and tags me before I can get back to the line beside the other boys.

Laughing and yelling, we put our arms around each other's shoulders.

"You were so fast!"

"Great throw!"

"I can't believe you got me! I almost made it." I say to Phát. Since I was tagged, I am now the keeper. Phát and I trade places, and we play the game for endless rounds. Sometimes I tease Phát by throwing my flip-flop at him instead of the can.

I haven't laughed like this in a long time.

While we play, I glance over at the sidelines and see

my mother with tears in her eyes. My heart freezes as I remember. This isn't a typical family visit.

***

On the night of the full moon, I'm told I'll be leaving in a few hours. I still feel as if the trip isn't really happening. At dinner, we celebrate my voyage with a feast of roasted pig, vermicelli and spring rolls.

"Eat more," my mother orders as she puts more meat on my plate. "You don't know when you'll eat like this again. Fill yourself up."

I eat so much my belly feels as if it might explode. Finally, when no one can eat any more of the main course, we each have an orange as a treat for dessert. I look around the table. The reality that I'm leaving starts sinking in and I wonder: *When will I eat a meal with my mother again? Or with my aunt and Phát? Or see my father and sisters back home?*

I excuse myself from the table and go to the washroom, even though I don't need to use it. I sit on the toilet, tears rolling down my cheeks. I listen to my breathing. In and out. In and out. I wipe away the tears from my face with my arm, not wanting my mother to know I've been crying.

As I head back to the dinner table, I overhear my mother and aunt talking in the corner.

"I pray to God the same thing doesn't happen to Thọ that happened to my friend's sons," my mother explains.

My aunt sounds alarmed. "What happened? Did they make it out?"

"No, their boat got caught just offshore. The older boy was jailed for over a year and hasn't been the same since he got out. Something horrible must have happened to him. Another friend's son's boat was also stopped soon after getting out to the open waters. They were all taken —"

My mother suddenly notices me. "Thọ, don't sneak up on me like that. Go eat some more food. You have a long journey ahead of you." Normally my mother would have scolded me even more. But my departure in a few hours has softened her. Even though I've been told to eat more, I can't. I sit, afraid to talk in case more tears come.

Later that night, my aunt hands me my plastic bag and leads Phát, my mother and me through the darkness to the back of the house, beside the river.

"We're taking a small boat to the bigger boat," Phát whispers.

"I'm coming too, aren't I?" asks my mother.

"Of course," my aunt says quietly. "We'll all go together and you can say goodbye when we reach the big boat." Then she adds, "No talking on this part of the journey. We don't want to give ourselves away." My aunt doesn't need to explain what will happen if we get caught. Many people have tried multiple times to escape from Vietnam and never made it out.

I am relieved that my mother is joining us because I am not ready yet to say goodbye.

Six other people appear from the shadows and scamper onto the boat. My aunt and cousin don't seem alarmed at their appearance. I don't know any of them, and no one makes introductions. I figure they are also going to the big boat.

Phát starts the boat's engine while my aunt motions for us to crouch down low on the floor so we don't attract attention as we charge down the river into the black tunnel of the night. The trees on either side of the river are so thick that their branches create a canopy above us, hiding the full moon. The boat's motor buzzes as loud as the mosquitoes, while frogs croak and crickets chirp from the shoreline.

I try imagining the big boat. I've been on several boats on the river, but I've never been on one at sea. I wonder what it will be like on a boat in the middle of the sea with no land on any side. I swallow hard, my mouth dry.

A shining light off in the distance moves toward us. Normally a light on the river wouldn't send shivers down my spine, but then normally I'm not escaping from my country in the middle of the night.

Phát must have also seen the light because he swerves the boat into the river's edge and turns off the motor, hiding us amongst the bushy shoreline. A gang of mosquitoes attacks me, but I refuse to attack them back with any slaps of my hand. Any noise might alert someone of our presence. Instead, I bite my bottom lip and hope the mosquitoes will stop biting me.

The large boat slowly passes. Fortunately, we aren't

seen. Phát waits until he is sure the other boat is long past before starting the motor again and continuing on our trek.

After what seems like an hour, Phát docks the boat. My aunt and my mother stay put while the rest of us climb out. I want to say something to my mother, but when I try to whisper a goodbye, my aunt shushes me. I don't even get a chance to hug my mother. I thought I would have time to say goodbye, but my hopes evaporate in the darkness. With a quick wave to my mother, I turn and follow Phát silently with the others, trying to blend into the shadows. My hand grips my plastic bag tightly.

A few minutes later, I see the outline of a boat. Phát whispers to a man standing by the boat and signals for me to get on board. My cousin gives me a final wave as I walk up the wooden plank and climb onto the boat. That's the last time I see Phát.

All I see on the boat are strange faces. I wish I could call out to my mother and yell goodbye or run back to her. The bright moon helps me see. I move until I find a space to sit down in the belly of the boat. It takes a half an hour or so for everyone else to board. With everyone on, there isn't room for me to lie down, but just enough for me to sit.

The boat leaves the shoreline and glides along the widening river toward the sea. It continues in the dark with the full moon stretching out a carpet of light for it to follow.

No one says a word. Eventually, the old man sitting beside me weeps quietly. "My wife ... oh my family." He cries a little louder until another voice nearby in the darkness hisses, "Shut up!" This silences the man.

I want to sleep, because it's late. Sleep will hopefully help me forget that I just left my mother behind and don't know when or if I'll ever see her again. I wish she were here, comforting me. I've never spent a night without her nor have I ever been out on the sea. All the emotions from leaving keep me awake.

Eventually, my eyes feel heavy, and I drift off. I'm not sure how long I sleep. The waves slapping the side of the boat make my eyes pop open. My head pounds. I start to sweat. I feel woozy. I want to lie down, but there is no room.

Suddenly, my dinner erupts from the pit of my stomach, shooting up my throat. Vomit spews from my mouth, covering my shirt.

CHAPTER 6

South China Sea

May 1981

"Thọ, are you okay?"

A familiar voice calls to me. It feels like it's been several hours since I threw up. I don't have the energy to open my eyes. I had been kept awake all night by people moaning, praying, crying and whimpering on the boat. I still feel sick. With no room to stretch, my limbs have fallen asleep. The boat rocks more gently now but it's not still enough. I want to be on solid ground. I want to be home.

"Drink this. It will help you."

A cup touches my lips, and I open my mouth. Someone tilts the cup and warm water rushes down my dry, raw throat.

I open my eyes and blink slowly, then rapidly in amazement. Here is Mai, crouching in front of me. The sun's rays shine on her beautiful face.

"Mai, what are you doing here?" I croak.

"Your mother told my mother about this boat. I overheard them discussing it one day when I was home from school with the flu. Your mother didn't have to pay as much for your journey if she could find other paying customers like my parents and me."

"Why didn't she tell me that your family would be on the boat?"

Mai shrugs. "Probably to protect us in case you got caught before getting on board. If that happened and you were asked if you knew of anyone else on the boat, you could honestly say 'no' and not give my family away." She puts the cool palm of her hand on my forehead. "How are you feeling? You look rough."

I look down at my T-shirt stained with vomit. The sour smell makes me feel like throwing up again.

"It's a good thing my mother gave me an extra shirt," I say. "I definitely need to change."

"Why don't you put it on," suggests Mai, "and we'll wash the dirty one out." She takes the cup and stands up, surrounded by a thick web of people.

I find my bag of spare clothes at my feet. With great difficulty, I shift my body into a position where I can change. Pins and needles poke my limbs as I move for the first time in hours.

I change into my only spare T-shirt, the one in which my mother has hidden the gold chain and my uncle's address. Finding Mai on this boat is a huge relief. I don't feel so completely alone without my family. Mai is a link to my family and home. I'm also happy her parents are on the trip. At least I have some adults to look out for me if I need them.

Holding my dirty shirt and bag in one hand, I get up

onto my feet. As I do, I accidentally step on someone's hand.

"ARGHHH! Have mercy on an old man!" I spring away, apologizing. This man is the same one whose weeping kept everyone awake the night before. I know I should respect my elders, but I am irritated. His whining made a hard time unbearable.

I manage not to trip over anyone else as Mai and I slowly make our way through the crowded boat. I shield my eyes from the scorching sun's rays. The smell of salt water overpowers the disgusting smell of my body.

I look around at my temporary home. The battered, wooden boat couldn't be any more than two meters wide and fourteen meters long, with a small cabin in the back where the captain steers. I watch a long-haired man with a thin mustache sitting down, huddled over and rummaging through something I can't quite see. His hand closes and disappears into his pocket.

From behind me, a man asks, "Has anyone seen my bag? A brown canvas bag?" I turn my head and face a man who looks my father's age.

Before I can answer, the man stops, a surprised look on his face. "Hey! What are you doing with my bag?" He points his finger accusingly. I turn my head to look and realize he is pointing at the man I'd just been watching. He straightens up, revealing a brown canvas bag beside him.

"I thought it was mine," the thief lies as he passes it to its owner.

I want to tell the owner of the bag to check and make sure nothing is missing. But the thief is glaring at me, his mustache drooping downward like a frown.

Mai and I quickly look at each other and then we continue inching through the tight crowd. As I pass a kid about my age, I make eye contact with him briefly and nod. He silently returns the nod. I follow Mai along the narrow space beside the cabin to a tiny area at the back of the boat. It's also crammed full of people looking sick, tired, hungry and scared. Near the stern sits a small stove where two women cook rice.

"There's over seventy of us crammed on this tiny boat!" says one of the women hovering over the stove.

"I'd feel a lot safer if there were half that number," responds the other.

Fastened to the back of the boat is a plank of wood with a railing around it — a makeshift toilet — with nothing below but the salty sea. A spare motor clings to the back.

I awkwardly maneuver past a weeping woman rocking her baby gently. The baby remains oddly still. In a panicky voice, she says to anyone listening, "I think he's dead! I gave him lots of cough syrup to make him fall asleep so he wouldn't cry and give us away. But he won't wake up. Is he dead?"

I gasp. I want to look away, but I can't. I have never seen a dead baby before and am surprised that it looks the same as if it was sleeping. I hear Mai call my name and am glad to move away from the woman and her dead baby. Mai is standing next to the stove, and I slide next to her. She has filled her cup with rice. "Let's eat something first," she says. "Then we'll clean your shirt." I drop my dirty shirt and plastic bag onto the deck near my feet. Then I grab a cupful of rice and sit down on the floor next to Mai, facing the water.

"I am starving," Mai breathes. She grabs some grains of rice in her fingers and gobbles them down. "Are you hungry, or do you still feel sick?"

"My stomach's still a little queasy."

"My parents are too sick to eat. But my stomach keeps growling." Mai smiles the same smile she often flashed at home. The boat may be small, but it's so crowded that I haven't seen her parents yet.

We sit in silence looking at the endless blue before us. As far as the eye can see, a band of blue water meets a band of blue sky.

"Oh!" Mai points just below us. Sleek gray noses break through the waves. Dolphins! Two curious dolphins swim around the boat, investigating it. Then they playfully dive over waves, arching over and under and over again, putting on a show before they skim away off to join some friends.

The dolphins make me think of my best friend. Lâm always talked about wanting to see one. I wish he was with us now so we could see them for the first time together.

"Hey, M-M-Mai," I stutter out of awkwardness,

dreading the answer to the question that follows. "What *really* happened to Lâm?"

Mai leans her chin over the edge as her smile drops down into the sea. Her eyes fill, and I hold my breath.

"He didn't make it," she says sadly. "Neither of my brothers did. We heard from a friend that there was a storm …" Mai hesitates. I stare at her face. "Some of the people on their boat were swept overboard and drowned, including Lâm and An."

I look away to stare at the unfeeling sea. Mai's news has ripped my heart from my chest. A wave of sadness engulfs my body. I can't speak. I want to cry, but I am too numb to do that either.

"That's why my mother wanted us to leave," continues Mai quietly. "She couldn't handle living in the house anymore. She kept saying that my brothers' memories haunted her there. She needed to get away from the house, knowing they'd never come home again."

Mai turns to me and puts her hand on my arm. But I am completely still.

"I wanted to tell you about Lâm. But I knew I couldn't risk the truth getting out."

Memories of Lâm race through my mind as I stare into the same sea that took him. Walking to school together each day. Running into each other's houses. Playing soccer on our street. Telling jokes that no one else found funny but the two of us. I think about the battles with our crickets. I wish Lâm had won that last cricket fight.

While I'm lost in my daydreams, the engine starts to sputter and quits. Mai wipes her face with both hands, and I swivel my head to see the captain and a few other men with creased faces, hunched over the engine. "Look," Mai says, pointing to the horizon. "Do you see that?"

"See what?" I respond, turning back to the endless water and sky.

"Over there. It's just a tiny dot."

Sure enough, I spot the tiny dot and watch as it gets bigger and bigger. It's a larger boat than ours, making a beeline toward our rickety vessel.

I jump to my feet and Mai gets up, too.

"This is great, Mai!" I cheer. "They're coming to save us. We're free!" I push all thoughts of Lâm out of my head. I just want to be off this boat.

The large boat slows down as it approaches our small vessel. Burly, serious men on board are waving machetes and knives. Although the men look scary, I am grateful, knowing I will soon be aboard their boat and heading safely for shore.

I look at Mai, who shrinks back from the edge, her eyes widening. "They're not coming to save us," she gasps. "I've heard about men like this. They're pirates, and we're being attacked!"

CHAPTER 7

South China Sea

May 1981

Within seconds, the pirate boat pulls next to our little one. Mai and I stand with the others, watching helplessly as some of the men — sure-footed and wiry — swing down a rope ladder and tie the two boats together.

Our tiny, feeble boat docked next to their large, sturdy one looks like a cricket next to a praying mantis. The hulking boat hovers over us with its high cabin in the back and large metal crane on the deck, reaching high into the sky.

"They're from Thailand," someone whispers behind me, though I have no idea how he knows.

Although only eight pirates appear, they carry themselves with the confidence of a large army. Dressed only in sarongs and headbands, the pirates carry shiny machetes or knives, and they look like monsters with white paint smeared on their faces. They shout at us in a language none of us understand. Even the long-haired thief looks scared. I hardly ever pray, but now I plead to God. *Help me make it, and I will try to become the best that I can be.*

The men yell and point their weapons at the women and girls on the deck, motioning for them to climb the ladder and board their boat. Standing beside me, Mai grips my arm with her fingers. She doesn't say a word, but her eyes look terrified.

"Don't do it!" our captain shouts. "Stay together!"

The women and girls follow our captain's orders and refuse to budge. Frustrated, one of the pirates grabs a crying baby by the heels and dangles her over the ocean. The threat works. The baby's father immediately screams, "Do what they say! Please don't let them hurt my child!"

Mai releases her fingers from my arm and silently joins the women and girls as they clamber aboard the other boat. The pirate passes the baby safely to its mother.

Two of the pirates drag the sick people who are sitting in the belly of the boat to their feet. As they move people around, the pirates check where people have been sitting to see if they were hiding any bags or valuables. For the first time, I see Mai's parents. Mai's mother looks pale and unsteady as she is forced up the ladder to the pirates' boat.

I stand near Mai's father along with the other men and boys on our boat and scan their faces. Even the bravest man can't hide his fear. Mai's father nods at me as if to say hello. He looks on the verge of collapse.

While some pirates empty our plastic containers of fresh water, upending them and peering inside, others make us open our mouths. They look for anything valuable we may have tried to hide.

I can see the women and girls on the pirate boat also having their mouths checked. One of the pirates yells at Mai.

I wish I were brave enough to bolt up the ladder, tear across the deck, and pull Mai from the screaming pirate. But I am too terrified. I stand rooted to our boat, fighting back tears and the fear that has seized me. Someone wails, "Please! Please don't yell at my little girl. She doesn't understand what you want!" I recognize Mai's mother's voice.

Back on our boat, the pirates grab every bag and dump its contents, picking through the small piles. They motion for anyone wearing jewelry or watches to take them off and put them in a bag that one of the pirates is holding. One pirate yanks a hat from a man's head and puts it on his own.

Suddenly, one of the pirates stops in front of the old man next to me. It is the same old man whose hand I stepped on earlier — the one whose moans had kept everyone from a decent night's sleep. The pirate mimes for the man to take off his wedding ring.

The man shakes his head. "Please, please," he begs, even though the pirate can't understand him.

The man puts his hands behind his back. The pirate angrily grabs the man's hand and waves a machete in his face, yelling something we don't understand.

"Give him the ring," a young man snaps. "He's

going to hurt you if you don't."

"It's all that I have left of my wife," the man sobs.

"He doesn't care."

I look into the pirate's eyes and my heart races. His eyes are glittering black stones.

Tears stream down the old man's face. Eventually, he raises his hands and tries to pull the ring off. It won't budge. The pirate motions to one of his friends to help him. A second pirate comes over and yanks at the ring. He isn't able to get it off either.

"Argh," the old man yelps, as the pirates twist and pull. Finally, they fall back, the first pirate clasping the ring to his chest. He pockets the ring as the old man crumples to the floor, crying. I look down at the old man. I want to comfort him, but I'm afraid to move. Meanwhile, the pirates gather up the loot and get off our tiny boat.

One by one, the women return from the pirates' boat. Weary and slow-moving, they climb down the ladder to the safety of our ransacked vessel. I breathe a sigh of relief as I see Mai safely on our boat. Her body shakes and her face is as white as a cloud. I look into Mai's eyes. Her sparkle left with the dolphins.

As quickly as they arrived, the pirates are gone. They leave our boat like a hurricane has struck it. I feel as if the air has been sucked out of me and I crumple down beside the old man. My heart thuds and thuds long after the pirates have gone.

For the rest of the afternoon and evening, the only

noises are the endless waves. The pirate attack has left all of us frozen with fear. Already hungry, stomachs rumble louder. The pirates have not only stolen our valuables but our limited food supply as well. With no food or water, we'll grow weaker. Our scrawny, ravaged boat drifts aimlessly. The men aren't able to repair the engine, and the pirates stole our spare motor.

In the afternoon, when I am dozing, I hear a happy cry. The mother who had given her baby lots of cough syrup is crying from relief. The baby is awake. But even that good news can't lift our spirits.

I hear people praying for a miracle. I think of my brother, Vũ, who survived his trip across the sea. Was his boat attacked by pirates, too? I think of my parents. They'd risked never seeing Vũ and me again in order to protect us. Who was protecting me now?

That night, I find a spot near Mai and her family and curl up next to them. But they don't talk to me or anyone else.

The old man's cries keep us all awake just as they did the night before. This time, no one yells at him to be quiet. Eventually the old man stops whimpering, and I manage to fall asleep. I awaken a few hours later to someone whispering: "He's dead." I curl up tighter and fall back asleep.

At daybreak, I watch some of the men drag the old man's body to the front of the boat. I try to act brave, as though I've seen a hundred dead bodies before. But inside I feel sick and afraid. The man looks lifeless just like the baby had — as though he is asleep and might wake up at any second — but, unlike the baby, he will not wake. The men lift the man's body onto a board and tie it securely with a rope.

Some of the women pray while I hear one of the men whisper to another, "We don't even know his name."

"Is he alone?" someone asks.

"Yes," another man replies. "After his wife died, he decided to leave Vietnam. He told me that the rest of his group was captured at a checkpoint and didn't make the trip. He'd left to go to the washroom and wasn't discovered. Somehow, he found his way to the boat. He was on his way to America to meet up with his eldest son."

The captain stands next to the body, a pen and ripped piece of cloth in his hand.

One man says: "Write on the cloth: 'We are seventy-six Vietnamese drifting at sea. Please rescue us.' We'll tie it to the old man and hope he's found."

"I don't know any language except Vietnamese," the captain says. "And no other Vietnamese boats are in any position to help us."

Instead, the captain writes "SOS" in large letters on the cloth and ties it to the old man's arm.

Then they lower the body tied to the board into the sea, while the captain says a prayer. The man's body floats briefly until a wave grabs him and pulls him, and the captain's SOS note, under the water.

CHAPTER 8

South China Sea

May 1981

After the old man's body disappears into the sea, people shield themselves from the intense sun with clothing, pieces of cardboard and whatever materials they can find. Stomachs growl. Tears chase tears. Heads bow in prayer. And I wonder what will happen to us. Will the old man's death be the first of many? I close my eyes and wish I was home.

Later that same day, another pirate boat comes. Like the first pirates, they separate the men and the women. This raid is quick and uneventful. These pirates are kinder than the first ones. They give us some sticky rice and steamed fish along with fresh water, which we quickly divide and devour after they leave us.

After a long, hot, boring day, I try to sleep at the front of the boat. Above, a million stars watch me. Though I close my eyes, I can't fall asleep. The noise of the waves striking against the sides of the boat keeps me awake. The cool sea air makes me shiver. As the wind howls in my ears, I open my eyes. From the dark sea, I think I see the old man's ghost, cackling and wailing.

I shut my eyes tight and cover my ears with my hands and try to imagine I am at home with the rest of my family. I pretend that I am in my living room, reading a book about Vietnamese legends. My favorite legend is the one about Sơn Tinh, the Lord of the Mountain, and Thủy Tinh, the Lord of the Sea. I have read this legend so many times that I know the story by heart and can even see the book's pages in my mind.

Many years ago, the king wanted to find the perfect husband for his beautiful daughter, My Nương. So he held a contest and the most powerful, intelligent and handsome man would marry his daughter. Many men throughout the land competed, but two men stood out amongst the rest: Sơn Tinh, the Lord of the Mountain, and Thủy Tinh, the Lord of the Sea.

The king asked both men to show off their special powers. Sơn Tinh explained that he was the Lord of the Mountain. He owned all the creatures and plants living on the mountain. When he raised his hand, he could make the mountains grow. The king was impressed.

Not to be outdone, Thủy Tinh told the king that he was the Lord of the Sea. He owned all the creatures and plants living in the sea, and when he raised his hand, he could make the sea grow. The king was so impressed with both men's talents that he challenged them to find the perfect wedding present for his daughter. The man who brought his gift to the king first would win his daughter's hand in marriage.

The next day, Thủy Tinh brought the king pearls from the sea as his wedding gift. Unfortunately for him, Sơn Tinh had come earlier, bringing diamonds from his mountains, and won My Nương as his bride. They had already run off to the mountains to marry when Thủy Tinh arrived with his pearls.

Thủy Tinh was angry that he'd lost the chance to marry the beautiful My Nương, so he lifted both hands and waved them wildly, raising the sea level higher and higher. But Sơn Tinh fought back and waved his hands wildly, causing the mountains to grow higher and higher. The two men battled for days until Thủy Tinh surrendered back to the sea.

But Thủy Tinh refused to give up completely. Every year people suffer while he seeks revenge against Sơn Tinh and his lovely wife, raising the sea levels and causing flooding on the land and up the mountains where Sơn Tinh and My Nương still live.

I look out to the sea. "Please don't hurt me, Thủy Tinh," I whisper before finally falling asleep.

In the morning, I slowly make my way through the crowd to the back of the boat. Near the cabin, I notice Mai squatting against the side of the boat, hugging her knees into her chest. She stares at a small picture of the Virgin Mary and mutters to herself. I haven't spoken to her since just before the first pirate attack. I try to get her attention, but her eyes don't leave the picture. I want to talk about home, but Mai clearly isn't in the mood to talk.

Suddenly, a woman shouts, "Look! There's land!"

"Oh no," one man groans. "What if it's Vietnam?"

Another woman replies, "If it's Vietnam, our lives will be worse than a hundred pirates raiding us."

"We'll be put in jail," the man agrees, "or worse —

sent to one of those re-education camps. No one ever returns from those camps."

I look at the dark shoreline peeking up from the blue horizon. My parents spent everything they had helping me escape from my homeland. I can't end up back in Vietnam.

Another pirate boat zooms toward us. It looks the same as the other two. The pirates leaning over the side of the deck look just as mean as the others. I pray again, hoping to survive this attack. I worry about what the pirates might do to us this time. Maybe they'll throw us into the sea after discovering there is nothing left for them to rob. I sit down, my palms pressing hard against the bottom of the boat, as though the pirates couldn't just tear me away and toss me overboard. I cannot swim particularly well.

These pirates don't have white paint on their faces. They wear nothing but shorts, showing off their muscular chests. The sun has darkened their skin. Like the others, they are probably from Thailand and don't speak any Vietnamese.

This time, instead of separating the women from the men, the pirates motion for everyone to board their boat. Our captain does not encourage us to rebel against the pirates like he did during the first pirate attack. Everyone quietly obeys and climbs the rope ladder to the deck on the pirate boat.

The pirate boat is made of wood like ours, but it looks sturdier and more seaworthy. Fishing nets and equipment lie in heaps around the deck. A large cabin sits near the back of the boat. Near the cabin is an open hatch with a steep, narrow staircase that goes down into the belly of the boat.

I lean over the edge of the pirate boat and look down at our frail, brown and blue wooden vessel with the numbers 555 painted on the side. Naturally, the pirates don't find any treasures on our barren boat. After finishing their pointless search, one pirate calmly says something to another one, who responds by nonchalantly shaking his head.

I have no idea where my bag of rice is or my other T-shirt and shorts. I also lost my flip-flops. I'd been taking them off whenever I sat cross-legged or to curl up to rest. I guess I forgot to put them back on at some point. The only thing that is still important to me is the T-shirt I am wearing with an American address for an uncle I've never met written on it and the gold chain sewn in the hem.

After the pirates search every corner of our boat, they beckon us to climb the ladder from their boat back down to our own. Before they depart, they give us a container of fresh water and some steamed fish and sticky rice. Then without smiles or a word, they tie our boat to the back of theirs, start their engine and tow us for a while until the land we fear is Vietnam disappears from the horizon. Eventually, the pirates untie their boat and vanish.

I spend the afternoon trying to escape the fiery sun

and savoring the water and some tiny pieces of fish as our boat drifts aimlessly across the sea.

Hours later someone points from the front of the boat and shouts: "Hey, there's a ship over there!" No one moves until he adds, "A big one!"

It can't be another pirate boat.

"Maybe it will save us!" I say excitedly to one of the men beside me.

"As long as it's not a Russian ship. We don't want the Russians rescuing us. They won't understand why we're leaving the Communists and might take us back to Vietnam."

In spite of our waving, jumping up and down and other attempts to attract the ship's attention, it doesn't move in our direction. It continues on its course until it disappears into the horizon.

I sink to the deck, feeling hopeless. With our boat's spare motor gone and its engine dead, we drift along with no power to move us forward. I've only eaten a few mouthfuls of food and have no energy. Even though I am on this boat that's packed with people, I feel completely alone. Mai and her parents still haven't recovered from the first pirate attack. No one would notice if I fell overboard.

Our captain doesn't have any maps. So even if we had a working motor, he wouldn't know for sure if land is a few days or a few weeks away. By that time, we might all have died from thirst or starvation. And no one seems to have any concept of where America is. It could be halfway around the planet for all I know. Even the one teacher on board has trouble explaining to me exactly where we might be.

How long can I go on like this?

CHAPTER 9

South China Sea

June 1981

I awaken the next morning to the sun's rays poking at my skin. Hoping to forget my hunger pains, I think of ways to survive this journey. I could swim to shore. Or ride on the back of a dolphin. Or build a raft from a few boards on this boat. Or flap my arms like a seagull and fly. Finally, I escape by letting my imagination take me home. I think of my mother and father. Then I close my eyes and watch a few duels between my crickets and Lâm's. My crickets win all of the matches, of course, although a few times it looks like Lâm's might taste victory.

Opening my eyes, I think of what I'd be doing if I were back home right now. It's a school day. I have no idea what time it is, so I don't know what class I'd be taking. I miss my friends at school. I even miss doing homework, something I never thought I'd miss! Before I have a chance to think of all the other things I miss about home, I'm interrupted by a man saying, "I've got an idea how to catch fish." I stand up and watch the man tie a small bone from yesterday's fish to a string.

Then he lowers the end of the string with the bone into the water, holding the other end. Hoping for food, a school of fish swim toward the bone.

As soon as the fish are close enough, two men lean over the side and scoop the fish into T-shirts they've turned into nets. They catch five large fish and two small ones. Enough for a few bites for each of us. They carry the fish, twisting wildly in their hands, to a woman who will cook them on the charcoal stove.

After the fish are cooked, Mai's father comes to me. Whenever I look at him, I think of Lâm. His father could be his older twin. He was always friendly and talked to me back home. But this is the first time he's spoken to me during our journey. "I brought you some food," he says and hands me a small piece of fish the size of my thumb. Then he sits down beside me, eating his own piece. "I've been really sick. This is the first bit of food I have had on the boat. I hope I can keep it down. Mai's mother is even worse."

Everyone on the boat gobbles down the fish. We lick the tiny fish bones clean, leaving no meat behind.

"Are you doing okay?" Mai's father asks me.

I don't have time to respond. Suddenly another pirate boat appears. None of us saw it coming. These pirates demand we all board their vessel just as the last pirates had ordered. Mai's mother has difficulty climbing the ladder. One of the pirates kindly helps her, as if he were her friend and not someone who wants to rob her.

I look around at our group. The raids by pirates are becoming routine, and we don't look as scared as we did the first time. But we do look hungrier and more beaten down as the days pass. Even though most of the pirates have left us with rice and fish, and we've caught a few fish on our own, there are so many of us that each person has only had a few bites of food since we boarded.

Are you doing okay? Mai's father's question rings in my ears. I am drifting on an overcrowded boat with no working engine that pirates raid regularly. My stomach is so empty that it is no longer grumbling from hunger, it's screaming. One man has died, and it's only a matter of time before someone else does, and I desperately hope that someone isn't me. *I am not okay*, I want to tell Mai's father. But I say nothing as we both peer down at our boat, watching the pirates.

The pirates don't find anything worthwhile, of course. Even though they look frustrated at the lack of loot, they still give us some fish, rice and water.

As I glance around the pirates' deck — cleaner, wider, sturdier than ours — a plan hits me. I can't believe I didn't think of it sooner. Though my pulse quickens, I take a deep breath. I need to think things over, and make sure this idea is solid. Something tells me this is not the right time to put my thoughts into action. These are not the right pirates. I need to be patient. I need to wait because the scheme could cost me my life. As soon as the pirates leave us stranded at sea, I spend the rest of the day rehearsing my idea in my head.

The next few days follow the same routine. Each day includes a pirate raid. Sometimes they leave us fish, rice or water after the attack. Most of the time, I go over my plan, weighing the pros and the cons. But I do not make my move. I'm too nervous.

The seventh day at sea brings another pirate boat. Once again, these pirates mime for us to climb onto their boat, while they raid our tiny vessel.

After we climb the ladder to their deck, we watch the pirates on ours. Unlike all the other pirates, these ones clown around as they check over our empty boat. They mime a fishing scene, pretending to fall overboard while pulling in their load. The others from my boat gather around the edge of the deck to watch the show. Some people laugh for the first time. Almost everyone is smiling.

While the crowd watches the pirates, I look around me. These funny guys must be fishermen — piles of nets and fishing gear are scattered around their deck. They also have a big crane on the deck.

The pirates climb back onto their boat and cook all of us sticky rice and fish for dinner. After we eat, the pirates give me and the handful of other kids a lollipop. I am excited — any pirates who give out treats must have kind hearts. These are the *right* pirates.

As we sit on the pirates' deck eating the food, the orange sun drops from the sky into the sea. Within a short time, we're sitting in the moonlit night with some light beaming onto the deck from the cabin. Everyone nods off to sleep. This is the first time we are able to stretch out after days squeezed in cramped quarters. I look around. The moon falls across the deck, creating shadows everywhere. I must be patient. I nod off, too.

After giving us the space to stretch out and sleep comfortably for a few hours, the pirates eventually wake everyone up and beckon for us to return to our boat. When the pirate nudges me awake, my eyes fly open. *I've lost my chance! Why did I fall asleep?* But as I look around, I realize my luck. The people shuffle slowly toward the ladder to climb back on our boat.

This is it! The sleepy crowd silently waits to file down the ladder. I slowly take a step backward into the darkness. Then another. And another. No one seems to notice me. After ten more careful steps, I am now standing away from the crowd. I look at everyone, hoping to see Mai one last time, but it's impossible in this darkness. With no one paying attention to me, I make my way to the open hatch and scurry down the steps.

At home, I loved playing hide-and-seek. I pretend I am at home now playing this game while searching for the perfect hiding spot. Unlike the games at home, I know if I am caught, the pirates might throw me overboard.

In the dark, I feel my way around. I find a crawl space near the engine and slide into it, lying on my back, covered in sweat and engine oil. The loud roar of the engine hides the noise of my pounding heart and heavy breathing. For once I feel lucky I am so small. If I'd been much bigger, I wouldn't have fit into the narrow space.

Then I wait. I count the seconds, then the minutes, then the hours. It's late, and I'm tired, but I'm too frightened to sleep. Twice in the night, I hear the pirates up on the deck. I keep waiting. If the pirates discover me, they might return me to my boat. The longer I wait, the better chance I have that the pirates won't be able to return me to my boat. I am not going back there. I have to keep moving forward.

I wait some more. My eyes are closed and I drift a little, but never completely fall asleep. My mind can't stop bouncing back and forth between good and bad thoughts. These pirates could seriously hurt me or throw me into the sea, and no one would ever know. But then I remember the lollipop and how the pirates made us laugh. These must be good pirates. At least, I hope that they are good, since I am hiding on their boat with nowhere to escape.

I am a cricket in a cardboard box, unaware of the fate that awaits me. When I eventually emerge, what will happen next?

CHAPTER 10

South China Sea

June 1981

My feet and hands are numb, and my fingers tingle. My stomach growls. But I can't hear it because all I can hear is the noise of the engine. It's time to go up.

Although I am terrified of how the pirates might react when they see me, I also know that I'll have to face them sometime. I might as well get it over with. It is difficult to move after being crammed for so long into such a small space. The engine's slimy oil covers my body.

I leave the engine room and slip up the hatch. When I reach the deck, I see a cook frying fish on a stove. He looks up at me, gasps, runs to the other side of the boat and disappears. I stand, shaking and sweating. *Why did I do this?*

The cook returns with seven other men. They gather in a semicircle around me, talking to each other. I do not know what they are saying. I study their facial expressions and how they speak. *Are they going to hurt me or help me?* I hope they don't notice my body quivering with fear.

Eventually the cook leaves the group. He returns and hands me a bar of soap. The men burst out laughing. I smile weakly and take the soap.

The cook ushers me to a hose on the other side of the deck. He motions for me to take off my clothes, which are drenched in oil from the engine. Gesturing, he indicates he will wash my clothes while I wash my filthy body. I scrub the oil and dirt from the top of my skinny body down to my toes. I'm clean for the first time since leaving home. I can't help but smile after the layer of dirt and grime has been scrubbed off my body.

When the cook finally returns, he has some clean clothes for me to wear. They are way too big. The cook drapes my clean T-shirt and shorts over the side of the boat to dry. Then he hands me a bowl of sticky rice and some fried fish. The flat, round fish has a beady eye that stares up at me. I grin back at it. The pirates wouldn't give me clothes and food or a bar of soap if they planned to throw me overboard.

I wolf down the food and wonder if anyone back on my boat has noticed I'm missing. I think of Mai and her family. They had each other to worry about.

Suddenly a gust of wind blows across the deck, picks up my clothes and throws them into the sea. I rush to the edge and watch my T-shirt and shorts floating on the sea's surface. Angrily, I slap my hands on the edge of the boat and cry "No!" uselessly in the wind. My gold chain is gone, as is my uncle's address written inside the shirt. I never memorized it.

I run to the cook, gesturing wildly to explain that I need to rescue my T-shirt. He doesn't understand why the T-shirt is so important to me and keeps point-ing to the one I'm wearing. *How can I explain about the hidden valuables?* A wave pulls my T-shirt and shorts down below the surface. I look away, sweeping my knuckles across my eyes. I stare at the sea on the other side of the boat. I'm in the middle of nowhere with nowhere to go.

For the rest of the day, I stick close to the cook, tour the boat and watch the pirates pull up the fishing nets and separate the fish every few hours. I try not to think about what I've lost.

That night, the cook finds a place for me to sleep. My stomach is full. My body is warm. My nose smells salty air and fish. For the first time since leaving Vietnam, I have a good night's sleep.

The next day, the pirates spend the entire time fishing. Each day follows the same routine. While the men fish, I spend hours looking out at the water, hoping that we don't see a Vietnamese boat. After another week at sea, I start to wonder if I will ever see land again.

I soon get bored. I have no one to talk to. The pirates are friendly, the cook feeds me, but we don't speak the same language.

The pirates keep all the fish in ice in multiple compartments beneath the deck. By the end of the week, the compartments are almost full. Once there isn't room for any more fish, I assume the pirates will head to shore. This is what I've been waiting for. I figured I would have a better chance of getting to shore safely on a pirate boat than the Vietnamese boat.

Finally, no more fish can be squished into the boat. I am ready for the next part of my journey and wonder where the pirates will take me next. Once we're on land, I hope that I find someone who speaks Vietnamese. I will ask them how to get to America.

Suddenly, the captain points to me and mimes having handcuffs on his wrists. I don't understand. I look around, and the pirates are all staring at me and shaking their heads. He turns on the radio and speaks in a low voice while another pirate sounds a horn.

Another boat, identical to this one, slices through the mist toward us.

CHAPTER 11

South China Sea

June 1981

The other boat comes close before cutting off its engine. The captains yell back and forth, and one of the pirates pushes me gently toward them. I think I understand now. The group of fishermen risk jail if they bring me to shore. I'm to go on yet another boat. The cook helps me, while the other pirates wave goodbye.

I fight back tears. *Is this my life now? Am I a pirate? Will I ever step on land again? Will I ever see my family again?* I climb easily over to the other boat. After the week of food and rest, my strength is returning.

These men are also fishermen. As we steer away from the other boat, I look around at the nets and ropes. I gesture to a nearby pile of gear, then point to myself. I repeat the signs, asking if I can help fish. I'm not going to be bored like I was on the last boat. These men also don't speak Vietnamese, so one of the men mimes the instructions.

A big net drags behind the boat. Every four hours throughout the day and night, the fishermen pull up the net using a crane and pulley. The machine guides the full net to the deck, where it dumps the fish.

My job is to help sort the fish. We separate the squids from the shrimps, the octopuses from the snappers. Each type has its own pile. They even keep tiny octopuses, their bodies the size of my thumbs, boil these in a pot and serve them for snacks. The fish feel slippery and slimy, and they twist and jerk in my hands, trying to escape. After we separate them, the fish are put in large compartments built into the deck, then covered with a layer of ice.

The fishermen keep every fish except the small sharks. They slice off the sharks' fins before throwing the finless creatures back overboard. It makes no sense to me, but there is no one to answer my questions. I can't help but stare at the finless sharks, slowly sinking to the bottom. I don't know why, but my heart sinks, too.

While I sort fish, I also keep my eye out for any Vietnamese boats. When I'm not sorting fish, I become the cook's shadow. The cook teaches me to take a squid, clean it, flatten it, then slap it on the smokestack to cook. Because the squids are so slimy, they easily stick to anything. Although I have eaten dried squid before, this is my first time eating roasted squid. It tastes delicious.

By the end of the week, I've become really good at sorting fish. The compartment is stuffed, and I know the fishermen will soon return to shore. I figure this means they will move me to another fishing boat.

The next afternoon, the captain beckons me to

follow him. We head to his cabin. Although I've explored most of the boat, I've never been to this room before. Mirrors decorate the four walls. I stare at my reflection and see how much I've changed in the weeks since escaping from Vietnam. The sun has dyed my skin a dark brown, and my hair is messy and scraggly.

The captain says "Papa" and "Mama" and gestures to me in a questioning manner. I think he is asking if I want to see my parents. I grin and nod vigorously, hoping this means I won't be sent to another fishing boat.

Reaching into a big bag, the captain pulls out a picture of the Virgin Mary and hands it to me. On the bottom of the picture someone has written in Vietnamese, "God be with you on your journey."

Then the captain leans out the door of the cabin and yells orders at two of the men. One of the men starts to flash the lights and sound the horn in a pattern. The other puts his hand on my shoulder and guides me from the cabin to the deck. While the boat zips along the sea, the cook runs around the boat collecting a dozen dried squid in a bag.

From the horizon, an enormous ocean cargo ship appears. The men all gather around me as the little fishing boat docks next to the massive ship. I stare up at the cargo ship, which is red on the bottom half of the hull and black on the top half. The words *Cap Anamur* are painted in dark letters on the side with the words *Port de Lumiere* in the center. I don't even try to guess what the words mean. I lick my lips and hug the bag of squid and picture of the Virgin Mary.

The cook touches my shoulder. I look up as he presses a beaded necklace into my hand. Another goodbye. I smile at the kind men around me and am startled when the cook gives me a hug.

Carefully holding on to my bag of gifts, I head to the rope ladder hanging down the side of the ship. I try not to look down into the sea below. After all the fishing I've done, I know what kinds of creatures live in it, and I have no intention of losing hold of the ladder and becoming their food.

As I step onto the ladder, I look straight ahead, carefully grabbing the rung above my head with my right hand. This hand carries the bag of gifts, so I have to be extra careful. Then I lift my right foot onto the next rung and take a deep breath. I slowly reach with my left hand and grip the rung above my right. When I feel secure, I lift my left leg. I move like this slowly up the ladder. One rung at a time. As I climb, my hands get sweatier and my knees get wobblier. I worry that I might slip. When I am close to the final rung, I tilt my head up and look onto the deck. I see a group of men leaning over the railing watching me. Some of them are holding fire hoses, aimed right at me.

CHAPTER 12

South China Sea

June 1981

One of the men helps me climb onto the deck and shakes my hand. He speaks a language I have never heard before. A Vietnamese man next to him pats me on the head and says, "Welcome to *Cap Anamur*" in Vietnamese.

"What's *Cap Anamur*?" I ask, relieved to speak my native language for the first time in two weeks.

"*Cap Anamur*," the man continues, "is the name of this ship." He sweeps his arm out wide, gesturing toward the vast deck. "It's run by a group of Germans who tour the South China Sea and rescue Vietnamese Boat People. We now have thirty-four Vietnamese refugees on board. They were rescued a few days ago. We were worried that your boat planned to attack us. This is a peaceful boat; we have no weapons. So, if the pirates you were with attacked us, we planned to hose them down. Those hoses are our weapons."

I feel the other people staring at me. The man explains that they are curious where I come from. "No Vietnamese travels with pirates, so we're wondering how a young boy like you ended up with those men."

My words burst forth as if from a broken dam. *Someone to talk to!* I explain my journey so far, from my parents' first attempt to have me leave with my brother to how I hid on the first pirate boat and then ended up on the second one. I finally ask my most urgent question, "Are you heading to America? I'm trying to get there to meet up with my brother and uncle."

The man chuckles. "We'll take you to a refugee camp in the Philippines. From there, the people who run the camp try to relocate the refugees to various countries around the world …" The man pauses and looks into my wide eyes. "Including America." He smiles kindly. "Now that you're aboard, we should know your name."

"Thọ," I say.

The man holds out his hand and shakes mine. "It's a pleasure to meet you, Thọ. My name is Huấn. I'm the translator on *Cap Anamur* and will help you get settled on this next stage of your journey. I was also rescued by *Cap Anamur*. You're in good hands."

As Huấn leads me below the deck of *Cap Anamur*, a huge smile stretches across my face. It's the first time I've smiled with joy since playing with Phát in Vietnam. While I am not on solid land yet, at least *Cap Anamur* is much closer to getting me to America. And this massive ship is much safer than any of my previous rides.

Huấn and I climb down a steep flight of narrow steps to the hold, a large open area with long strips of sleeping mats on the floor. A few people are sitting and chatting on the mats. It seems most of the people on board are still gathered on the deck. Ropes of colorful and tattered laundry decorate the steel walls.

"Here's where you'll sleep," Huấn says as he points to one of the mats with a blanket, pillow, toothbrush, plastic bowl, pair of chopsticks and towel on it. "You can leave that here if you'd like," he adds, motioning to the bag of gifts given to me by the pirates: the dried squid, the picture and the necklace.

I reluctantly put my bag on the mat, unsure if I can trust any of the people on this ship.

"I've got a T-shirt and shorts for you." Huấn hands me a shirt and a pair of jean shorts. "You can change into them now if you'd like. Your clothes look like they're pretty big on you."

I especially like the new T-shirt. It smells clean and it fits, unlike the fisherman's shirt that I'd been wearing. The shirt is white with a picture of an anchor on the front with green and red letters above it.

"*Cap Anamur*," says Huấn, pointing to the words on the front of my new T-shirt. "The captain is Rolf Wangnicks. But everyone calls him 'Papa.' He was the man who shook your hand and welcomed you aboard.

"We'll pick up as many people from boats as we can over the next few weeks. When we're full and need more supplies, we'll stop on an island called Palawan. That's where a refugee camp is. It's where everyone will disembark."

I nod silently and repeat the word *disembark*. At last! I'm not going to live at sea forever.

"You'll live at a camp until you're relocated to America or one of the other countries accepting refugees." Huấn leads me back to the deck. "I'm here if you need anything. I won't join you at the refugee camp, but I'll be here for your entire time on this ship. Papa hired me as a translator but also to take care of everyone. Are you hungry?"

I think of the bag with dried squid back at the mat and shake my head. "No thanks. I've got some food with me."

"I can tell you've been treated well on the other boat. You don't look nearly as starving as most people when they first embark. Dinner is served in a few hours. You line up over there." Huấn points to a place on the deck with a long, white counter. "Bring your bowl and chopsticks with you." He keeps walking. This boat is much longer and wider than my street back home. We haven't yet reached the other side. Then we head back below the deck, down another set of stairs.

"Our next stop is a room called the hospital. A doctor checks all the Boat People when they arrive. The benefit of you being the only one from your boat is that you don't need to wait in line to see the physician." We stop in front of a doorway blocked by a folding table and a woman sitting behind it. She doesn't look at me, only addressing Huấn and writing on a clipboard.

Huấn turns to me. "You're brave to travel this journey on your own, Thọ. Okay, here's the doctor. I'll stay with you to help translate."

The hospital consists of a large room with rows of canvas cots. The medical check doesn't take long. I am healthier than most of the Vietnamese Boat People, thanks to the good care from the pirates and fishermen. As the doctor checks my ears and mouth, I think of Huấn's words: *You're brave to travel this journey on your own.* I *have* been brave. And lucky. But how much longer do I have to keep being brave? How long will my luck last?

Huấn sometimes asks me to turn or open my mouth wide or look into a small flashlight, but mostly he and the doctor ignore me as they talk. I think of Vũ. Is he still brave and lucky?

Then I think of the people on the first boat — Mai, her parents, the men, women, boys and girls. I hope they are still alive. Maybe the crew on *Cap Anamur* rescued them.

After the medical examination, I mention Mai and her parents' names to Huấn and ask him if they've been on board. He doesn't recognize the names but promises to look at his records.

From the doctor's office, Huấn leads me back to the deck and takes me over to a mother and her son, who looks about my age. We check each other out from the corners of our eyes.

"Thọ, I'd like to introduce you to Việt and his mother," Huấn says. "Your sleeping mat is next to theirs. Since you and Việt are the same age, I thought you might like to meet each other." Việt smiles at me, and I return it. A Vietnamese boy my age! Finally! "I better run and help Papa. I'll leave the three of you to get acquainted."

"Are you traveling by yourself?" Việt's mother asks after Huấn has gone. "I saw you boarded the ship alone."

"Yes," I say, "I was on a boat with other Vietnamese but got separated from the group."

"We were on a boat with thirty-two other people," Việt explains. "My mother and I are hoping to get to America, where my father lives with my older brothers and sisters."

Việt rubs his stomach.

His mother says, "Việt, you need some rest." She turns to me and explains, "Việt's not feeling well. He should lie down for a while. Perhaps you can join us at dinner."

I am disappointed not to run off and explore the ship with my new friend. I watch as they head to the sleeping area. I have lots of time before dinner, so I wander across the deck in search of Huấn and find him with Papa on the bridge.

Papa is staring into a pair of binoculars at the endless field of blue water. The captain hands the binoculars to Huấn with a hiss in his voice. Something has upset him. I look out at the sea where he was frowning.

"No!" the translator barks in Vietnamese as he focuses the binoculars. "Those blasted pirates. They've got a boat." Huấn gives me the binoculars. Through the lenses, I see a pirate boat flying along the surface of the sea and towing a decrepit Vietnamese boat behind it. The fast-moving pirate boat causes waves to spill over the sides of the helpless Vietnamese vessel. The Vietnamese on board cling to the sides of their boat as the rough, angry sea tries to take them.

CHAPTER 13

South China Sea

June 1981

I watch the terrible scene, my heart hammering. *People on their boat were swept overboard and drowned.* I hear Mai's voice in my head and try not to picture Lâm and An's last moments.

Papa shouts orders. *Cap Anamur*'s siren blares, along with repeated blasts of the horn. I wince, but I can't cover my ears. I grip the binoculars, bracing my feet as the massive ship turns swiftly and charges, surprisingly fast for its size.

The pirates, realizing *Cap Anamur* is chasing them, increase their speed. Then I spot two more pirate boats joining the one towing the Vietnamese vessel. The three boats look like a gang of bullies preparing to fight a smaller kid at school. *Cap Anamur*'s engines roar as they are pushed to their limit. Realizing the massive ship is gaining on them, the two latecomers break away and begin circling *Cap Anamur*.

Huấn shouts to me, "Keep an eye on the Vietnamese boat and call me if something happens to it."

The crew arm themselves with parachute flares.

They intend to fire them if the pirates attempt to board or attack our ship.

The German ship finally catches up to the first pirate boat, which floats a few meters from *Cap Anamur*, staring up as though it is taunting the Germans to fight.

Papa blasts the horn and siren again and again. The crew raise their arms, ready to fire flares at the pirates. The pirate boat responds by revving its engines. It appears as though a battle is about to begin, when suddenly one of the pirates unties the rope connecting the Vietnamese boat to his own. Then the pirate boat races toward the other two boats. The three vessels disappear into the horizon in search of their next victim, leaving behind the crumbling Vietnamese boat barely floating on the water.

"They're safe!" I shout as I look down at the group of terrified faces on the boat below.

While the crew rushes into position, adrenaline pulses through my body. A few of them hurry down the rope ladder to the refugee boat below. They help the women and children board a special rescue platform in small groups. Each group is carefully pulled up to the deck.

Huấn leans over the railing and speaks through a megaphone. As the waves slap the side of the half-wrecked boat below, he calls out to the people still on board, "Stay seated and spread apart or you'll tip!"

I should feel only happiness and relief as I watch dozens of women, children and men safely climb aboard. But I don't. No one cheers or celebrates. One woman weeps and thumps her chest. The rest look exhausted and in shock. Even though the sky is blue, I feel like dark clouds hang over every Vietnamese boat escaping from our homeland. I wish that I had the power to remove the imaginary dark clouds from the sky. Looking around the group, my body quivers. *What if we hadn't saved them in time?*

I wonder how many more Vietnamese will join *Cap Anamur* before we land in the Philippines and if all the rescues will be as dramatic as this one. And I wonder if all will end as well.

***

There isn't much to do in the weeks that follow. The only excitement occurs when we save five more Vietnamese boats, adding a few hundred more refugees to the German rescue ship. But these rescues aren't as eventful as the first one.

I spend most of the time playing with Việt.

"Let's play tag. You're it!" Việt shouts to me as he runs toward one of the large yellow cranes on *Cap Anamur*'s deck.

"I'm tired of tag," I grumble. "That's all we ever play. Let's play something else for a change."

We sit on the deck trying to think of something different to play. Since we have no soccer ball or cans or sticks to play with, we are left with games like tag and hide-and-seek.

"Let's have a cricket fight," I suggest, wishing I were at home with my kingdom of crickets.

"How can we do that when we have no crickets?" Việt laughs.

"Why don't we pretend we're crickets, then? And we can fight each other."

"Yeah!" Việt exclaims. We face each other, crawl on all fours, raising our back legs and rears like the large back legs of a cricket ready to hop and jump. We hiss and chirp as crickets do in the heat of battle. Việt laughs easily and, encouraged, I act sillier. Suddenly, I am yanked sideways.

"Boys! Boys! Stop that!" Việt's mother has pulled us apart. She doesn't understand the rough games boys sometimes play. "You shouldn't fight each other."

"We're not fighting. We're pretending," Việt explains, jumping up and down, ready to resume the battle.

Việt's mother wags her finger and says, "Well, I don't want to see pretend fighting or real fighting. Besides, you need to rest, Việt. You can't afford to have another attack."

Việt's mother is always worrying about his health. Although Việt sleeps a lot, he seems healthy to me. He also never complains about feeling sick. I figure his mother is overprotective.

We sigh and go back to sitting around and doing nothing.

***

Around midnight, I awake to Việt moaning in pain. "Shhh, shhh," his mother soothes.

Emergency lights keep the room dimly lit. I turn on my side and look at Việt. Sweat glistens on his pale forehead and cheeks. His hands grab his stomach in pain. His body is curled on its side with his knees up to his chest. Việt's mother is bent over him, gently wiping her son's brow with a shirt.

Hearing me turn, Việt's mother whispers sharply: "Please, Thọ, hurry and get a doctor. Việt needs help."

I jump up from my mat without asking any questions and run along the narrow passageways to where Huấn sleeps. I need him to translate to the doctor.

"It's Việt," I say in a panicked voice, as I shake Huấn awake. "He's not well. He needs a doctor quickly." Huấn and I run to the hospital, where one of the doctors is checking on patients. Huấn explains the situation to the doctor, who wastes no time rushing to Việt's sleeping mat.

After a short examination, the doctor decides my friend needs to be moved immediately to the ship's hospital so he can better diagnose him. With the help of Huấn, the German doctor wraps Việt in his arms and swiftly carries him to one of the cots in the crowded hospital area. Việt's mother and I follow them, but when we get to the hospital, Huấn sends me back to bed.

"There's not much you can do, Thọ," the translator explains. "Go back to bed and get some rest. Come and see Việt in the morning. He should be fine by then."

I try to peer around him into the room, but he closes the door.

Back on my mat, I try to sleep but can't. I stare at the metal ceiling and worry about my friend. That worry leads to all the rest of my worries, and I think of my parents and my sisters. I think of Vũ. Where is he right now? Did he make it to America? I pretend my brother is sleeping beside me and we are in our living room. Eventually I fall asleep.

***

First thing in the morning, I go back to the hospital to check on Việt. But the doctors shoo me away. Another Vietnamese boat has been rescued that morning and the doctors don't have time or room for healthy people like me hovering around. Only Việt's mother is allowed to stay by his side.

I spend the day pacing the boat and eavesdropping on conversations. Finally, at dinner, I see Huấn in line getting food and rush up to him.

"How's Việt?"

"He's not well," Huấn responds. "He's going to stay in the hospital tonight. If he hasn't improved by tomorrow, we've radioed for a helicopter to come and pick him up and take him to Singapore for surgery."

"What kind of surgery?"

"He's having problems with his appendix and may

need to have it removed. Let's hope and pray he improves today and won't need the surgery."

I thank Huấn and walk sadly to the back of the line.

***

The next morning, I awake to a thunderous noise above. A helicopter!

I race to the stairs. I know what this means.

I stand with a crowd on deck, all of us a safe distance from the terrible wind and noise coming from the blades. It's thrilling to see a helicopter up close, but then I see two men carrying a stretcher and I take a step forward.

White sheets cover Việt from his chest to his feet. I want him to look over at me so I can wave goodbye, but Việt's eyes stare up toward the clouds. Việt's mother follows the stretcher. She is crying.

The helicopter's rotors blow everyone's hair, and the roar of its engine fills the air. The helicopter lifts and flies off toward the horizon. I watch until it looks the size of a bug and eventually disappears.

CHAPTER 14

South China Sea

July 1981

The day after Việt is flown to Singapore for emergency surgery, I wake up to the ship rocking. The small boat that I left Vietnam on swung back and forth with the waves. So did the two pirate boats. But until now, *Cap Anamur* had been strong and steady.

I climb to the deck, where the wind howls and the rain drenches me. Waves the size of hills rock the ship to the right. I grip the railing hard with both hands. When the ship tilts to the left, I lose my grip and fall onto the deck. Clutching the railing, I pull myself to my feet. Then I stagger along the deck, grabbing the railing for help. I find safety on the bridge, where Papa controls and steers the ship. There, I join Huấn, who is looking out a window at the wild storm.

"This storm is brutal." I state the obvious. My hair and clothes are soaked from the short time in the rain. Huấn doesn't respond.

"Have you heard any news about Việt?" I ask a few moments later, breaking the silence.

"Not yet," answers Huấn, "But I'm sure he'll be

fine. He's in good hands. He's much luckier than many other people are right now."

I look at Huấn, not sure what he means.

"Most of the Vietnamese at sea aren't in boats that can survive this kind of storm," Huấn explains. "Sadly, many of them will likely drown today." He rests a hand on my shoulder. "Consider yourself lucky, Thọ. You made it to *Cap Anamur*, and you're alive. And I'm confident that Việt is going to be all right as well."

I suddenly cry out. The violence of the waves, the noise, the power of the sea — this is what Lâm and An faced. I feel small facing this storm, even on this great ship. I can't imagine what they must have felt in a small wooden boat. I cover my face with my hands. I wish *Cap Anamur* was around to save them.

Huấn puts his arms around me to calm me, asking, "Is it reminding you of someone?" I nod, not saying a word. Huấn hugs me tight and whispers in my ear, "Me, too." We both cry in silence, finding comfort in each other.

Finally, Huấn pulls out of the embrace and says, "Let's go down below to the hold. Papa is addressing everyone there soon and needs me to translate."

"What's he telling us? Are we going to the Philippines today?" I ask, rubbing my eyes. *Cap Anamur* is close to capacity, which surely means we will go to the camp soon.

"You'll have to wait and hear!" Huấn yells over the roaring waves and wind, as we leave the bridge and slowly make our way across the deck. Huấn helps guide me across the deck and into the hold, where the crowd has gathered, waiting for the captain's address.

At last the crew silences the group. Papa speaks a few words, and Huấn translates.

"I know you are all anxious to land in the Philippines and begin the next phase of your journey. This ship is overcrowded, and you're all living in cramped quarters. I appreciate that these conditions are not ideal. However, I am asking for your patience. We will not be docking for a few more days. The crew and I are on these waters to save as many lives as possible. That is our duty. We want to give the Vietnamese boats escaping across the South China Sea right now the same opportunity that all of you have been given. I promise we will land in the Philippines within the week, but I need you to understand that —"

A voice calls out over some speakers, interrupting the captain's speech. I don't understand the words, but I know they mean another refugee boat has been spotted. Huấn hurriedly yells that the captain will share more later, but we can all see the time for talking is over. Another boat needs rescuing.

We are all aware of the storm outside and know we are lucky to be alive. The announcement of a found boat is also a reminder of our good fortune. As we wait in the hold during the rescue, I hear Huấn calling out instructions through a megaphone. I don't need to see the boat to know it is packed with more people than a boat should handle. And no one on board will have eaten a meal in days. It will also look as if one large wave could flip it over. All the Vietnamese boats look the same.

Slowly the rescued people are brought into the hold. I overhear one of them telling Huấn, "We haven't eaten or had fresh water in two days. If this ship hadn't come along, we would have either drowned in the storm or starved to death."

One newly rescued man walks unsteadily down the stairs, as hands reach out to help him. When he gets to the hold, his shorts slip from his skinny waist to his ankles. He tries bending down to pull the shorts up but has no energy left even to do that. There was a time at home when I would have laughed at this. But not now. Now this sight makes me angry and sad.

The man collapses. Two of the crew rush to his side. They lift him onto a stretcher and carry him to the hospital.

Most of the eighty new rescues are too weak to walk to the hospital. Some people are carried on stretchers and others in the arms of the crew.

***

The next day I get up early and wander up to the deck to see Huấn. The storm has ended, and Huấn is watching the sun rise.

"How are the people who arrived yesterday?" I ask.

Huấn doesn't respond and continues staring at the sun.

"Are the people from yesterday's boat okay?" I ask louder, thinking Huấn may not have heard me.

"Most of them didn't make it through the night," Huấn says quietly. "The doctors did everything they could. But we found them too late."

My eyes fill with tears. I don't even know these people. I want to go home. I want this journey to end.

Huấn senses my sadness and puts his arm on my shoulder. "It's at times like this," he says, "that I feel blessed to be alive."

CHAPTER 15

South China Sea

July 1981

Huấn beckons me over at breakfast.

"I have something to show you when you finish eating," he says.

"What is it?"

"It's a surprise."

I quickly finish my baguette in record time. Huấn then leads me through the ship toward the hospital. He gently pushes me through the doorway.

"Việt!"

Việt lies on a cot, propped up against pillows, eating his breakfast. His mother is sitting on a chair next to him, a huge grin stretched across her face. I rush to his side. When I get to the bed, his mother jumps up and squeezes my shoulders. I am not sure if she's hugging me or protecting her son from me.

"Hey, I think I know you," I tease. "You didn't think there was enough fun on this ship, so you took off?"

"Yeah, but I was even more bored at the other hospital, so I thought I'd come back and torment you," Việt jokes. His mother laughs at our teasing.

"So, you're okay?" I ask, suddenly serious. I peer at him closely.

"Yes. It was no big deal. I'm missing my appendix, but I'll be fine." Việt smiles. I sit next to my friend's cot, and we talk for hours. I am surprised Việt and his mother weren't sent from the hospital in Singapore directly to a camp. I am glad I have my friend back.

The following evening, Việt and his mother rejoin me in the sleeping area on mats next to mine. Việt's return comes with some other good news.

"We're landing in the Philippines tomorrow morning on an island called Palawan," Huấn announces after dinner to the more than 400 Vietnamese on board. "After we land, buses will take you to a refugee camp. A group from the UNHCR will meet you there and interview each of you before you settle."

The crowd of people buzzes enthusiastically at this news.

"What's the UNHCR?" shouts a voice over the crowd's rumblings.

"The United Nations High Commission for Refugees. It's the group that runs the camp and will help get you placed in one of the countries accepting Vietnamese refugees."

The excitement of finally getting off the boat makes it difficult for me to sleep that night. I lie awake, thoughts swirling in my head. *What will the camp be like? Will there be many people there? Will I make friends there? How long will I be there?* For one brief second, I imagine finding Vũ there. But I just as quickly bury the thought. Some hopes hurt too much.

***

The next morning, I grab my plastic bag. Inside are my few belongings and some of the dried squid that the cook gave me. I have been barefoot since losing my flip-flops on the first boat, so I don't have any sandals. I wear the T-shirt from *Cap Anamur*, a pair of jean shorts and the colorful beaded necklace I was given.

Then Việt and I race up to the deck. His mother runs to catch up with us. One by one, we file past the lineup of doctors, nurses and crew members. I hug Papa and Huấn.

"Thank you" — I grin at Huấn as he releases me from the hug — "for everything."

"You're welcome, Thọ. I wish you well on the rest of your journey."

More people to say goodbye to on this endless adventure. The thought of finally reaching land makes my heart fly. So why does it also feel anchored to this deck?

Việt and his mother hug some of the doctors. Members of the crew rip off their T-shirts and wave them as our group marches down the gangplank to the dock. After spending two months at sea, I hope this ship is the last one I'll be on for a long time.

People laugh and whistle, clap and sing as we move

another step closer to freedom. It feels like a party. The closer we get to the dock, the more the crowd presses forward. Việt and I weave through the pack.

"Boys!" Việt's mother yells after us as she tries to keep up. "Boys, wait for me. We've got to stick together. Boys!"

Finally, my feet hit the shore. The sound of my bare feet slapping the hot pavement as I run makes me smile. *What a relief to feel solid ground again.*

Việt's mother finally catches up. After lightly scolding us, she guides us onto one of the many buses taking us to the refugee camp. She sits in an aisle seat with Việt next to her and me by the window. I am keen to see the Philippines. As I press my face to the window, I realize I am glad to see anything other than water.

The bus takes us down a main road. Within a short time, the houses and buildings disappear until there is only the occasional one. Tropical trees and plants line the roadway. So far, the Philippines looks just like Vietnam. About ten minutes later, the bus parks on the side of the road near a metal fence. Slowly, the group on my bus exits and joins the mass of people from the other buses in front of the refugee camp's metal gate.

We walk down the dirt road into the camp. Crowds of the camp's current residents stand on either side of the road, curious to check out the latest arrivals and see if there's someone they know. The crowd is thick and moves slowly. Laughter and shouting rings in my ears. A voice calls instructions over a loudspeaker.

Việt, his mother and I follow the others along Palawan's main road toward the building where we'll register and get instructions on where we'll stay. Before we get to the building, we pass a church with a cross in the front.

Just after I walk past the church, I hear a high-pitched scream from the crowd. Before I can turn my head, someone rushes toward me, wraps a pair of arms around my waist and squeezes tightly.

"You're alive! I can't believe you're alive!"

I wriggle away and turn.

CHAPTER 16

First Asylum Camp, Palawan

July 1981

"Mai!" I gasp in astonishment. "Is that really you?" We hold each other by the shoulders. Mai's grip is strong. Her skin is dark from the sun and her long hair is even longer.

"It's me all right." She grins. "But is this really *you*, Thọ? I thought you were dead."

"Yes, it's me, and I'm definitely not dead."

"What happened to you? We thought you fell overboard. The captain even prayed for your soul." Mai's eyes are dancing again the way they used to back at home. "I can't believe you ended up in Palawan — out of all the places in the world! My parents are going to be shocked."

I can't believe Mai is alive! And her parents! This probably means that the people on my original boat made it. Before I can ask, I feel Việt tap me on the shoulder.

Mai and I let go of each other, and I introduce her to my new friends. I tell her that we plan to stick together at the camp.

Mai greets Việt and his mother and says, "I'll bring you to where you get registered and assigned a barrack. After that, I'll take you to my hut. My parents will be so happy to see you, Thọ!"

"Can we request to move into a hut instead of the barracks?" Việt's mother asks.

"You have to pay for a hut to be built," Mai explains. "Or you can buy one from a family that's leaving."

Mai leads us to a large one-story building at the end of the main road in the camp. We line up with the other residents of *Cap Anamur* to register and receive a few supplies. I ask Mai how to send a letter home to tell my parents that I am safe.

I can't stop smiling. This is already so much better than a boat!

After we register, one of the camp volunteers — a young woman, maybe in her twenties — takes the three of us to our barrack. Mai tags along as well. As we walk out of the main building, the volunteer points across the road. "See those two gray concrete buildings with the blue metal roofs?" she asks. I look to where she's pointing. All the buildings are concrete with metal roofs, but only two have blue roofs. "That's the school. You can take English classes there," she says. A priest walks out of the church beside us. "Hi, Father," our tour guide waves. The priest smiles and waves back.

When we walk past another building that looks similar to the school, the volunteer explains, "That's where you line up for food. Behind that building is the main water station. There's a few of them around the camp." The mention of water makes me thirsty. The sun feels extra intense, especially with no trees in the camp for any shade.

As we continue walking, the volunteer directs her comments to Việt's mother. She is very chatty. Maybe that's why she volunteered to greet newcomers. "The camp is only two years old. About half the people live in barracks. My family started out living in a barrack, but it's so crowded. As soon as we had some money sent, we had our own hut built. We've been in it for a month now, and I'm much happier. If you decide to get one built, let me know, and I can recommend the guys who built ours." Before Việt's mother has a chance to respond, the volunteer adds, "The camp even has a jail." Việt and I look at each other and our eyes widen. "Anyone who causes serious trouble is sent there for a few days. But don't worry. We've only had a few people stay there since I arrived six months ago."

Many people walk past us during our tour. But I don't feel nearly as crowded as I did on the boat with Mai and her parents. The crackle of the loudspeakers occasionally breaks through the noise of people laughing, children playing and babies crying.

"Every morning they play a short clip of Mozart from the speakers as a wake-up call," the volunteer explains. I want to ask who Mozart is, but before I get a chance, she stops in front of a building, "There's your barracks. Let's go inside and I'll show you where you can put your sleeping mats."

Mai waits for us outside while the volunteer, Việt, his mother and I walk through the door. The large room is almost as big as the hold on *Cap Anamur*. Giant bunk beds line the walls on both sides. People sleep on the bottom or top level, with their head against the wall and their feet toward the center.

The volunteer takes us to an empty section on the lower level. "This is your area here," she says. We each put our sleeping mats down on the wooden structure. Then she points to some markers on the floor. "They indicate the space for every two people." Judging by the distance of the markers, we each only get an area a little bigger than our sleeping mat.

"As you can see," she adds, waving her hand toward a set of towels hanging from a rope, "some families separate their sleeping areas by hanging towels. You can do that if you like. Is there anything else you need?"

The three of us shake our heads.

"All right, I better get going. I've got more newcomers to help get settled."

Leaving our sleeping mats and stuff behind, we follow the volunteer out of the building. She heads back toward the main office, and we follow Mai to her hut.

As we weave our way along various dirt paths through the camp, I look at everything. I am still marveling that I am on land. That I am safe. When we pass one of the barracks and turn a corner, I almost collide into a man.

"Watch where you're walking!" the man snaps.

He gives me an evil stare. I instantly recognize the long hair and thin mustache. The thief!

"You almost ran right into me," the man continues. He takes a menacing step forward. I back up, right into Việt's mother, who takes my shoulders and steers me around the thief, murmuring, "Sorry, sorry." I can feel him watching us.

Finally, Mai points to a hut in the far corner of the camp, next to a large fence. "Here we are," she says. The hut is made out of skinny tree trunks no wider than my arms and has a roof of coconut leaves.

Mai breaks into a run. "Look who I found!" she calls.

Mai's father stands up abruptly from a wooden bench and knocks it over. He looks at me as though he's just seen a ghost. Coming down the ladder from the loft, Mai's mother shrieks. She climbs down faster, practically jumping off before wrapping her arms around me. "We thought you were dead!"

Then she pinches my arm. "Ouch!" I respond, even though the pinch doesn't hurt too much.

"Not a ghost!" she laughs.

We are laughing and talking at once. I introduce Mai's parents to Việt and his mother. Mai finally breaks in, "You still haven't told me what happened to you, Thọ!" We all sit around their table, and I tell them about my journey: my plan, escaping on the pirate boat and *Cap Anamur*.

"You're lucky to be alive," Mai's father declares.

"Yes, lucky indeed," echoes Mai's mother. "And isn't it wonderful that you've ended up at the same camp as us. Your mother asked me to keep an eye on you, and I despaired that I had let her down when we lost you. But this truly is a miracle."

"Let's celebrate that you've safely rejoined us and welcome our new friends," announces Mai's father. We cheer and spend the next hour chatting. As Mai and her mother cook, they tell us about their journey to Palawan.

No one had realized I was missing until the next morning. Then, assuming I'd been swept overboard in the night, the captain conducted my funeral. When Mai describes this part, her voice grows soft. A few days later, a ship that sounded as big as *Cap Anamur* rescued them and brought them to Palawan. If I'd stayed with them, I would have reached land seven weeks earlier. I shake my head at myself.

Finally, dinner is ready. The six of us sit on the benches in the hut and eat the delicious meal of rice, fried fish and green beans. *Cap Anamur* food was mostly dried or canned. A hot, freshly made meal is heaven, and I stop talking to focus on eating.

Mai's parents ask Việt's mother about their journey. She tells them that her husband escaped two years ago with her eldest son. Her next three older children escaped last year. They are all currently living in

America, where Việt's mother hopes she and Việt will go and eventually reunite with their family.

We eat the rest of the meal in silence, thinking of our families both far away and gone for good.

After dinner, Mai takes us to the communal washrooms.

As we get close to the wooden stalls, I can smell their stench. I am about to walk into one of the open stalls when a long-haired man steps in front of me and cuts me off.

"Hey!" I protest, letting him know I was there.

The man snarls and turns. "You got a problem?" It's the thief again. He walks into the stall and shuts the door.

I stare hard at the closed door. *Yes, I do have a problem.*

CHAPTER 17

First Asylum Camp, Palawan

July 1981

A few days later, Mai's mother sends us kids to the beach to collect some snails and seaweed for snacks. Mai's mother will dry the seaweed and then boil it to make a jellied treat.

We all grab buckets and Mai leads the way, since Việt and I have not been there yet. We zigzag through the camp, through the gates, turn left on the road and run barefoot to the beach. When we arrive at the beach, no one is around. The shoreline isn't very sandy. It's mostly covered with tropical trees and plants.

Mai and Việt instantly run into the water, but I stop suddenly on the shore. The waves look gentle, licking the shoreline. But I know first-hand how quickly the sea can change into a wild beast. I walk slowly into the shallow water, turning my head a few times to see how far the shore is.

Suddenly, I jump up and down. Mai and Việt, several meters away now, look back and laugh. We kick the water, whooping and laughing. The sea is wonderful now that I can feel land.

I catch up to Mai and Việt in a patch of green seaweed. It looks like long grass, swishing back and forth to the rhythm of the waves. Underneath the seaweed, I step on something slippery and slimy. I look down and see what looks like a black, rotting cucumber. As I pick it up, it slips out of my hand and I jump. "It's alive!" I gasp.

Mai laughs. "I could have told you that!" Then, she shows us which snails to pick and how to catch them. The snails her mother wants are jumping snails. We have to move quickly to catch them as they spring from one piece of seaweed to the next.

Before picking snails, I pick half a bucket full of seaweed. After catching some snails, I throw them in my bucket on top of the seaweed, and then go to catch some more. When I add more snails, I discover the first snails are gone. This continues a few more times until I realize that the snails are leaping out of the bucket!

Near me, I hear laughter. Mai and Việt are bent over howling while watching me.

"Put the seaweed over the snails." Mai giggles. "That way they won't jump out." I follow Mai's instructions and laugh along with my friends.

We decide this beach is our secret place. Mai explains that hardly anyone is ever there, so it feels like our own playground.

***

The next morning, we head to the beach to fish. Mai's father has given us some string and two hooks. Mai plops down on the shore as Việt and I wade out in the water. I watch a seahorse rock slowly in the shallows, its tail curling and swinging from side to side like a cat's. Việt and I wade out deeper. We have each tied a string to a stick and put a hook at the end of it. Before dropping the line in the water, we catch a tiny fish with our hands. We stick it through the hook and use it for bait. Then we drop the hook in the water. We fish until we have enough for dinner. We haul the bucket back to Mai before Việt runs back out to the water for a swim.

Mai watches as I fill the bucket with water before gently placing it in her shadow. Then I sit down next to her to take a break. She watches the fish wriggling around for several minutes before tracing her fingers around in the sand. She does this when looking for shells. I already see a small pile in front of her.

Eventually Mai breaks the silence: "Sometimes when I find a really pretty shell, I want to show Lâm or An. Then I remember I can't." I want to say something, but a lump gets caught in my throat.

"I wonder where they are," Mai continues, "and if they're okay."

I clear my throat, unsure if I can speak. After a beat, I croak out, "I think they're riding dolphins across the sea, and playing soccer in the clouds and fighting crickets."

Mai forces a small smile. "I hope you're right."

"I hope Lâm has lots of crickets. And that he's winning all his fights."

"I'm sure he is. I'll bet he has already won hundreds of crickets."

"He probably has so many crickets that he doesn't know what to do with them," I add. Thinking of Mai's brothers makes me think of mine. I wish Vũ were here sitting next to me on the beach. I take a deep breath and hold it in.

We are so far away from each other. The first night here, I wrote a letter to my parents, but I haven't yet heard back. The man in charge of mail said it might take close to a month. I imagine them seeing my handwriting. I wonder if my mother's eyes will get misty. My father's won't. But he'll read the letter many times. I had asked about Vũ and hoped they would send me good news. And an address.

From the water, Việt hollers our names and beckons us to join him. Mai gently squeezes my arm. "Thank you, Thọ," she says. We each wipe our eyes with our hands. Then we grab a bucket and race into the water to join Việt in the middle of a patch of seaweed. For the next hour, I search the water for different creatures. I find strange, dotted rocks and pick them up. I am startled when I realize that they aren't rocks, but creatures that quickly retreat inside their shells, trying to hide from me. I collect more, hoping to ask the teacher at the camp's school to identify them. I try to find another of the black cucumber-like creatures, too, so my teacher can help me learn about it. But I can't find one.

As the sun rises to its peak, we collect our buckets and head for Mai's hut. Her mother is walking out of the hut as we arrive. She admires our shelled creatures but is very excited to see all the fish.

"We will have a lovely dinner tonight. Thank you, kids," Mai's mother says. "Việt, your mother has some errands for you to do. Mai and Thọ, we need some fresh water. I was going to ask your father to get some, but he is volunteering today. I'll get you some empty buckets."

With a bucket each, Mai and I wander off to an open area with a faucet.

Mai and I glance at each other as we near the water station. The thief from our boat and one of his buddies are here to "supervise." The sun is intense today, and there is a lineup at the water station.

"Come on, let's move it. It's hot out here," complains one man standing in line ahead of us. The thief, a cigarette dangling from his lips, crosses his arms, raises his eyebrows at the man's comments and saunters over to him.

"What'd you say?" the thief barks, his eyes piercing into the man's.

The man doesn't flinch or look flustered. "I said,

'Let's move it. It's hot out here.'"

"What's your name?"

"That's none of your business," the man replies, obviously unafraid, even though he is much shorter than the bully.

"It *is* my business." The tormenter beckons for his friend to join him. "Hey, Quỳnh," the thief calls. "This is the guy you told me about, right?" They both turn to the man. "Your name is Huy, right?"

Huy stares straight ahead and ignores the question. I gaze at the ground and shift from one foot to the other uncomfortably. Mai stands beside me and glares at the two tormenters.

Quỳnh walks up to Huy. "You were on my boat. Do you recognize me? You came when we were boarding and threatened our captain that you would alert the authorities if he didn't let you join us.

"On board you laughed and bragged about how you scammed a spot and didn't have to pay." Quỳnh puts his nose right in the man's face. "That's who you are, right?"

Huy neither speaks nor moves.

"Minh, this is the weasel." The thief, Minh, takes a few steps closer to the two men as Quỳnh continues. "You're not getting water. I spent everything I had to get a spot on that boat. Everything! You think you can get a free ride? If you want water, you can pay for it!" Quỳnh yells, pushing Huy so hard that he is forced to take a step backward. Minh jumps beside Quỳnh.

The lineup of people quickly circles the three men.

"Fight! They're gonna fight!"

I am frightened for Huy, although I'm impressed he doesn't cower.

Minh pushes Huy, harder than Quỳnh had, and he stumbles backward, falling on his rear. Minh then raises his fist, ready to plow it into the man's stomach.

"STOP IT! STOP IT! STOP IT!" screams a voice next to me. Startled, I turn.

Mai steps from the circle of observers and walks toward the three men.

"He may not have paid for his spot on the boat," she snaps, "but maybe his scam was his only way out. Does it really matter? Obviously, he wanted out of Vietnam, just like the rest of us. So, leave him alone."

The two tyrants look stunned at being talked to like this by a tiny, teenage girl.

At that moment, two of the camp staff and a volunteer arrive on the scene. Someone had run to warn them of a fight breaking out at the fresh water station.

"What's happening?" the volunteer asks.

None of the three men speak. The crowd remains silent. After a tense minute, Mai jumps in. "There's been a misunderstanding. That's all."

The staff members decide whatever has happened isn't worth the bother and return to their office. None of the men will be arrested and spend any time in the camp's jail.

Once the staff have left, Minh and Quỳnh take off, too. The group quietly resumes its line. Huy gets up, his back very straight, and calmly fills his bucket full of fresh water.

"Mai!" I take a deep breath. "You really stood up to those jerks."

"I'm done with being scared," she explains and then helps me fill our buckets.

The next day, Mai and I line up for food before realizing we are right behind Minh. I freeze as Huy walks up in line behind us. I widen my eyes at Mai, who sticks her chin out.

When Minh collects his food, he turns around and slips Mai an extra tin of peas. Neither of us react. But as we step up to collect our food, I hear Minh snarl at Huy, "We're not done with you yet."

CHAPTER 18

First Asylum Camp, Palawan

September 1981

One day, my name is called over the loudspeakers to go to the office. When I arrive, I am given a letter. I know immediately it isn't from my parents. The handwriting on the envelope isn't theirs. I check the name on the top left corner. It's from Vũ! Finally! The return address is from a country I know little about: Canada. I run to the barrack and huddle on my sleeping mat. I hold Vũ's letter, flipping it over in my hands. I read the return address a few times. An old woman stares at me from the stamp on the top right corner. I turn the envelope over one last time and rip it open.

Dear Thọ,

Mother sent me your address. I am so happy that you have arrived safely in the Philippines. A lot of people who try to escape aren't as lucky as we are.

I spent over a year at a refugee camp in Malaysia. From there, I tried tracking down our uncle in America. But I wasn't able to find him. Then I heard about a Canadian teacher who had sponsored some Vietnamese kids like us who had escaped without their parents. His name is Bryan. He agreed to sponsor me.

I have been living with Bryan and three other refugee kids for a few months now. I am really happy. I love living in Canada. It's very different from Vietnam. It has four seasons. The other kids tell me that in winter it gets so cold that you have to wear gloves or your fingers will freeze. I hope you end up in Canada. Then we can see each other again.

Write to me. I miss you.

Love, Vũ

I read the letter twice. Vũ is alive. Vũ is safe and alive! But he couldn't find our uncle in America. I don't know anything about Canada. I flop backward on the mat and stare up at the metal ceiling. Vũ didn't share details of his time at the refugee camp. Or what it was like on a plane. Or what our parents wrote to him. I finally had some answers, but now I had even more questions.

***

A little while later, Việt's mother comes in to rest on her mat. I sit up. "Do you know where Canada is?" I ask her.

"I hear it's very far away — near America," she says.

I sigh and slump back down.

"Why do you ask?" she adds.

I hand her the letter and explain that it's from my brother. "This is good news!" she says, handing it back to me after she's finished. "Thọ, this is such a blessing! Why do you look sad?"

"Because Vũ is living so far away now, and I don't know if I'll ever see him again." Tears prick my eyelashes.

"I believe you will see your brother again and your parents and sisters, too. Be patient. It will happen."

"Do you really think so?"

"I know so," she says, but I'm not convinced. I turn over and bury my face in my arms.

"My brother is so lucky that he's not in a refugee camp anymore." I can hear Việt's mother get up from her mat and sit beside me. She places a warm hand on my back.

"You are lucky, too, Thọ" she says quietly. "Not everyone who leaves Vietnam makes it this far. Trust me. You won't stay here forever, even though I know it feels like you will some days."

***

Later that afternoon, I borrow a pen and paper from Việt's mother and write a letter back to Vũ. The next morning, I stop by the office to mail the letter before heading to English class. I wave to Mai, who is volunteering there today.

Then I join Việt in our English class. Miss Knox

points to a list of English words on the blackboard and says, "Classroom."

"Cassoom," repeats my class, struggling with the weird letter combinations.

"C-L-A-S-S-R-O-O-M." Miss Knox points to each letter as she pronounces the word slowly.

"Classroom," we repeat.

"Window." She points to the next word on the list and then to the small window through which a sunbeam shines a spotlight on the young Scottish teacher's face.

"Wi-d-d-oo." We stumble over the W sound. It's not a letter that we have in our language. I am frustrated with the number of letters in most English words. Vietnamese words are short and simple to speak. Many English words are long, and pronouncing them feels like I'm speaking with a mouthful of pebbles.

I know I should keep trying. English will help me in either America or Canada — if that's where I end up. But today I can't focus on a faraway dream. I don't want my tongue tied in knots while trying to repeat these long, strange words. Today is Tết Trung Thu, and I can't wait to escape from this classroom and celebrate the mid-autumn moon.

Halfway through the lesson, Miss Knox claps her hands. When we quiet down, she draws a picture on the blackboard and says, "Moon." The class smiles. Miss Knox knows today is special to us and understands why we are having difficulty concentrating. She dismisses us early, and we hurry back to our temporary homes, eager for the moon to light up the night sky.

"I wish we had some moon cake to eat," Việt says. "I always loved eating moon cake back home."

"I don't miss moon cakes as much as I miss having a lantern," I reply. Back home before Lâm left, the two of us would go to the market before the Moon Festival and buy a lantern each. I wish we were there now, dressed in colorful costumes and masks, carrying our lanterns. We marched through the crowded streets loudly singing songs. Our frog, butterfly, fish and flower lanterns lit up the night. I always bought a dragon lantern.

At dusk, Việt and I join a stream of children who parade through the camp, singing. The group makes its way to the open area near the school, where a group of adults organize stories and games. I'm surprised to see Huy is one of them.

We gather around in a circle as Huy tells us a legend that I used to hear back home during Tết Trung Thu. "There once was a lumberjack named Cuội," he says. "One day while collecting wood in the jungle, he came across four tiger cubs playing. Cuội killed the tiger cubs with his axe. Shortly after, a noise startled him. It was the cubs' mother. Afraid, Cuội climbed a big banyan tree.

"The tiger saw her dead cubs and immediately ripped some leaves from the banyan tree, chewed them and gave the leaves to her cubs. The cubs immediately sprang back to life and they took off with their mother.

"Once it was safe, Cuội climbed down the banyan tree. Realizing the banyan tree had special powers, Cuội dug up a smaller banyan tree to take home with him and replant in his garden.

"On his way back home, he came across an old man dead by the side of the road. Cuội picked some leaves from the banyan tree he was carrying and did what he had seen the mother tiger do. The leaves worked and Cuội brought the old man back to life. The old man asked him what had happened, and Cuội described what he had done.

"'The banyan tree has special powers,' the old man explained. 'It can bring people back to life. But you must take good care of the tree, and always water it with clean water. If you water it with dirty water, it will float up to the sky.'

"Cuội took the banyan tree home, replanted it and was always careful to water it with clean water. From that day onward he saved a lot of people with his banyan tree's leaves and word spread about his special power.

"One day, when he was crossing a river, Cuội saw a dead dog floating in it, and he used the leaves to bring the dog back to life. Grateful, the dog followed Cuội everywhere and became his best friend.

"Then a rich man in a nearby village came to see Cuội because his daughter had drowned. He begged Cuội to bring her back to life. Cuội did and, as a reward, the old man agreed for Cuội and his daughter to marry.

"They lived happily until some bad people, who were jealous of Cuội and his special powers, came to their home. They played a trick on him and killed Cuội's wife. They took her guts and threw them in the river, so her body wasn't whole and Cuội couldn't easily save her.

"Cuội was devastated. He tried bringing his wife back to life but failed. The dog, seeing his master so helpless, offered his own guts to replace the guts in his master's wife. Cuội took the dog up on his offer and used the dog's guts to replace his wife's, and then he used the banyan tree leaves to bring her back to life.

"After she came back to life, Cuội's wife wasn't the same and became a little forgetful. Cuội had to remind her to water the banyan tree with clean water. But she forgot, and she peed next to the tree.

"Immediately, the tree started to shake. Its roots pulled up from the ground. Cuội rushed home in time to see his tree floating away. He grabbed the roots and tried to pull the tree back to the ground, but the tree floated all the way to the moon with Cuội still holding on.

"And that is why, when you look up at the moon, you see different shadows and shapes. They are the banyan tree and the lumberjack and —"

"— and if he is not careful, he's going to fall from the moon and crash into the ocean!" A man shouts from behind the crowd. I do not need to turn my head to know who is interrupting Huy's story. I groan silently. Minh ruins everything.

His friend Quỳnh shouts, "So you see what happens if you climb trees."

"All right, kids," Huy says to us kindly. "We're going to play some games. Line up to play Bite the Carp's Tail."

I jump up. This is one of my favorites. All the kids line up in the same direction, holding each other's waists. Việt is in the front of the line, pretending to be the carp's head, while I am at the end of the line, as the tail. Huy tucks a piece of cloth into the back of my shorts. When Huy yells go, the other kids in line swing right and left, trying to protect my tail as Việt tries to grab the cloth. The game ends when Việt, as the carp's head, grabs the cloth from my shorts.

Just after we start, I feel the cloth ripped from my shorts. "Hey!" I shout, turning around. Our line quickly breaks apart as we all let go of each other. Minh holds the cloth up high with his signature smirk aimed at Huy.

"That's enough. Let the kids have their fun," Huy snaps.

"The kids are having fun watching me *whip* the carp," Minh shouts. He snaps the cloth like a whip as he charges toward Huy, who runs away in the direction of the camp office. The staff there will protect him.

We all scatter, racing back to our barracks to hide from the thugs, leaving the fat, bright moon to celebrate the festival on its own.

CHAPTER 19

First Asylum Camp, Palawan

October 1981

A few weeks after the Moon Festival, I'm walking through the camp with Việt, carrying a large net that we have borrowed for fishing. We don't talk. It's early and we don't want to wake anyone. Việt suddenly grabs my arm and pulls me to one side of the path. Before I ask what he's doing, I see his face. I look where he is looking, wide-eyed, and see Minh and Quỳnh stomping toward us. Minh carries a knife, and Quỳnh has a machete. They storm past us.

I turn to watch them and see someone walking out of a hut. *It's Huy!* We realize at the same time what is about to happen.

Mai was able to stop them from hurting Huy once, by screaming, but that felt different. This time they have obviously planned. There will be no swaying them. I silently beckon Việt. We hide behind a nearby hut. Suddenly, I hear a piercing scream. My heart hammering, I peek from behind my hiding place and see Huy on the ground, wailing as blood gushes from his leg.

Soon half a dozen people are running toward the scene. The whole camp has woken up. They surround Minh and Quỳnh, backing them against one of the huts. They yell for the men to put down their weapons. Quỳnh waves his machete in the air and slices it through the bamboo wall of one of the huts. A woman inside screams, pokes her head outside and throws a bottle into the crowd. The bottle hits one of the men who is trying to help. That man picks up a small cooking stove, lifts it over his head and throws it at the hut, smashing it through the wall. The husband of the woman grabs the man and starts punching him.

Suddenly Minh and Quỳnh aren't the only ones fighting. Several men now join the brawl. Others come out of their huts with rocks and sticks, while others carry knives.

Việt and I crouch down together, making ourselves as small as possible. Someone shoots a string of laundry into the air like colorful fireworks. I want to help Huy but there is no way to get to him safely. One man pushes another man toward Việt and me. We jump to get out of the way.

Huts crumble from the weight of bodies and objects thrown against them, and the bamboo sticks from the huts' walls become weapons. I can't make out what anyone is yelling. People's screams and shouts sound as loud as thunder crackling.

Suddenly, the camp staff arrive, blowing their whistles repeatedly. As they start prying people apart, I notice Minh and Quỳnh slinking away behind one of the huts, trying to escape. I motion to Việt to follow me.

I pick up the net. Việt and I follow the thugs on a parallel path. We run faster than they do, and get ahead of them. As we race across the back of a building, my heart races. My mind races. I imagine my crickets preparing for a battle, puffing their wings and chirping loudly. Trying to anticipate my enemies' move, I figure that Minh and Quỳnh are going to come along the side of the building momentarily. I hand Việt one side of the net and direct him to stand on the other side of the path, while I pick up the other side of the net and stand across the path from him. We stare at each other in silence.

At last we see the two men. We raise the net and they run right into it. Startled, the men fall down, and Việt and I pull the net over them.

"Hey! HEY!" Minh yells, "What are you doing?" He and Quỳnh flap their arms, trying to escape. But this only tangles them in the net even more, like insects in a spiderweb.

Việt and I yell for help, and two camp officers come running. They untangle Minh and Quỳnh from the net, slap a pair of handcuffs on each of them and take them away.

"You're a hero!" Việt slaps me on the back. "That was a great idea to catch those jerks with the net."

"I'm not sure about being a hero." I smile. "But I have learned a lot about fishing. I just pretended those thugs were big, nasty sharks."

Talking excitedly, Việt and I return to where the fighting began. Our jaws drop. The area looks as if a typhoon has swept through, destroying everything in its wake. Laundry, bamboo and roof thatching litter the ground. The Palawan staff have the battle under control. I look around at the damage. How could this happen?

The refugees spend all afternoon cleaning up. No one talks. No one apologizes. People who had thrown their fists at each other earlier are now helping each other rebuild their huts. I work with a group cleaning up the garbage. Fortunately, no one is seriously injured, although Huy and some of the others require stitches.

Mai, Việt and I help after school, making faces at one another but otherwise not fooling around. As I gather broken bamboo into small piles, I look at the adults' solemn faces. The desperate, haunted expressions from the boat are gone, but I see something I had not noticed. Everyone is sad. Everyone is slumped with exhaustion.

This is no home.

Mai's father invites me, Việt and his mother to dinner. After a quiet meal, Viet's mother clears her throat. "I have some good news," she says. "Do you want to hear it?"

We lean forward.

"Yes! Tell us! What is it?" Mai, Việt and I say in unison.

Việt's mother turns to her son. "We are leaving the camp for good. Next week, we're going to America and rejoining our family."

CHAPTER 20

First Asylum Camp, Palawan

October 1981

"I'm not going to miss your snoring," I tease.

"Just wait until you hear my father's." Mai laughs.

I sit in the wet sand with my two friends for one last time. My voice is light and friendly, but inside I ache. I want to be the one leaving. In a few hours, Việt and his mother will leave the camp for Manila. From there, they will board an international flight to join Việt's father and siblings on the other side of the world.

I know that I should be happy for Việt and his mother. They've waited a long time to be with the rest of their family. I should also be grateful. At least I have Mai and her parents. I am moving into their hut from the barracks after Việt and his mother leave. It could be worse. I could be *completely* alone.

I pick up one of Mai's shells and toss it into the sea.

"Hey!" she protests.

"Let's not talk about me leaving," Việt decides. "I want to play in the ocean one last time."

The three of us jump to our feet and bolt into the waves. Water sprays us as we run. We dive in, tasting the salty sea. Việt stays under longer than Mai and me, pulling the water with his arms, kicking his legs, swimming underwater as far as he can until his body needs air. Coming to the surface, Việt has swum a good distance away from us.

"Come back!" Mai calls to Việt.

"In a minute!" yells Việt, as he flops on his back, bobbing on the surface, staring at the sky.

***

Back at Mai's hut, we eat one last lunch together. After, as a special treat, Mai's mother gives us each a bottle of something called Mountain Dew and some peanuts. I have never had anything like Mountain Dew before. The sweet drink dances on my tongue. We talk about how much better life is going to be in America for Việt and his mother. I smile broadly, but my heart sinks to my feet. As a goodbye gift, Mai lets Việt choose some shells she collected.

"Just think," Mai's mother says, "you won't have to share a toilet with hundreds of people." We all laugh.

As we clean up after lunch, Việt disappears. At first, I assume he's gone to say goodbye to some of our friends, but when he doesn't appear after a few minutes, I go looking for him. I finally find him at the beach, sitting under a palm tree and looking out at the endless horizon. I am surprised to discover that Việt has been crying.

"Việt, are you all right?"

His red swollen eyes stare at me as I tower over him.

"Don't tell anyone I'm crying, okay?" Việt pleads.

"Of course I won't. What's the matter?" I sit down next to him.

Việt takes a moment before responding. "What if I don't like America, Thọ? What if I don't make any friends? What if I'm the only Vietnamese kid in my class, and I can't understand anyone's English? How am I going to make friends if I can't even speak to them?"

The firing of questions makes me dizzy. I don't know what to say. I hadn't expected him to feel this way.

"You're going to live with your father and your brothers and sisters, right?"

Việt nods.

"And they've been living there for a while, right?"

Việt nods again.

"So, you've got family who will take care of you. They'll make sure you never feel alone. Families are like that. They take care of each other."

Việt stops crying. But suddenly I feel like crying. I am alone. And I am tired of being alone.

I remember the faces of the refugees after the fight. I close my eyes and think of what Huấn from *Cap Anamur* said. *You're very brave.* But when will I leave this place? And will my whole family ever be together again?

We sit silently for a long while.

Finally, Việt gets up and brushes the sand from his shorts. He pulls me up with one hand. "Race you back to the camp."

"I bet I'll beat you."

"In your dreams." Việt laughs.

He beats me easily.

Back at the barracks, Việt, his mother and I collect our few personal belongings. While Việt and his mother say goodbye to Mai's parents, I drop off my bag in Mai's family's hut. We go back to our barracks one last time to make sure we haven't missed anything. Then together we all walk to the bus. Several other refugees are milling around it, saying goodbyes and talking to the camp volunteers.

I feel a lump in my throat. Mai's eyes mist over, and Việt drops his head in sadness. Even though this goodbye has always been inevitable, we don't want it to come.

Before boarding the bus, Việt turns to Mai and me as we stand on the side of the road and says, "You'll have to come and visit me in America someday."

"Maybe you'll have to come and visit me here, if I never leave," I declare.

"Or wherever I end up," Mai adds.

"Maybe we can meet somewhere in the middle," Việt suggests and hugs each of us quickly before boarding the bus. We wave and wave and wave until the bus is out of sight.

CHAPTER 21

First Asylum Camp, Palawan

June 1982

Vũ sends me letters at least once a month. He describes the leaves on the trees bursting with colors before they all fall off. He tells me about seeing snow for the first time and sliding down a snowy hill on a thing called a Crazy Carpet. He also tried to ski down a hill in the winter and gave up after he kept falling on his butt. He describes the snow melting and the ground changing from white to green, and the leaves returning when winter turns to spring. I love hearing news from my brother about his new home. But reading the letters also makes my heart sad. He always asks if I am okay. When he learns that I am with Mai and her parents, he tells me that he's relieved I'm not alone, that I have someone from home looking after me.

Every day in Palawan feels the same. At the beach, sometimes big, ferocious waves crash onto the shore. Other times they're small and gentle, slowly crawling along the sand. The size of the waves might change, but my routines at the camp don't. I still spend as much time as I can at the beach. I catch fish, investigate new marine life and wade through the water. Each week I eat the same food. Line up in the same lines. Take the same English class. And play the same games over and over.

Each day I listen intently to the messages that are sent via speakers throughout the camp. I often go to church on days other than Sunday and pray that, like Vũ, someone will sponsor me and take me out of the camp. I tell the priest that I hope by praying directly from a church, God might hear me better and respond faster. But each day passes with no news.

How much longer will I be living in Palawan?

One night, almost a year after I arrived at the refugee camp, I am sitting in the hut with Mai and her parents after dinner. The wind howls outside.

PLOP. A raindrop lands on the coconut leaf roof. PLOP. PLOP. PLOP. The wind gets more intense. Suddenly, I feel a raindrop land on my head. Then another, and another.

Some raindrops must have landed on Mai's mother, too, because she announces, "There's a hole in the roof! I'm getting wet."

"There's more than one hole," I say. "I'm getting wet, too."

"Same here," Mai exclaims.

We grab whatever buckets and containers we can find and place them on the floor to catch the water.

After we've done all we can for the night, we go to bed. I try to fall asleep, but I can't. I lay awake listening to the wind and the rain as the drip, drip, drips hit the buckets. *I miss my family. I miss Vietnam. When will I ever leave this place?*

By the morning, the storm has passed. The dirt floor is muddy in spots where we missed putting a bucket. Mai's father leaves to find someone to help him repair the roof. Mai and I collect the buckets and containers with water in them and dump them outside.

As usual, music hums from the speakers. But I don't find the beautiful sound comforting the way I used to. I eat my breakfast, not looking forward to another day of disappointment. After breakfast, I walk to the beach with another boy from the camp to fish. He doesn't talk much, so I don't either.

An hour later, I hear Mai calling from the beach. I am in the water up past my waist. She jumps up and down, waving at me to come.

"Tho," she yells as I approach. "They've called your name to go to the main office."

"Maybe there's a letter waiting for me." That's the main reason my name gets called.

"It can't be that. Mail delivery doesn't come until tomorrow." Mai grins. I could see my hope reflected in her face. "Go right away. It might be good news."

I drop my fishing line on the sand and run. My legs pump as fast as they can back to the camp. Mai trails a little behind me. I don't want to get my hopes up. Maybe the message has nothing to do with me leaving Palawan. My name might have been called for a different reason. As I pass the South Vietnamese flag, it gently waves to me.

When Mai and I rush into the office, the UNHCR staff and the translator greet us with huge smiles.

"Thọ! We know you've been waiting to hear about leaving the camp," the volunteer translator says.

"Yes, sir," I say. Whenever I pick up a letter, I ask if there's news about me being sponsored and leaving.

"Your brother's sponsor, Bryan, applied to sponsor you, too. The good news is that the application has been accepted. Thọ, you're going to Canada to live with your brother. Even better news — we've got you on a flight to Manila tomorrow. You'll stay at an intern camp there for a week before flying to Canada. Your time in Palawan is over."

I ask him to repeat it. And then again. He laughs but does what I ask. The news is so unbelievable. I am moving to Canada! I am going to live with Vũ!

Mai gives me a hug. "I'm so happy for you, Thọ. You're finally leaving here."

I squeeze her back and we jump up and down in the office until one of the volunteers laughingly tells us to give him back his office. We race to the hut to tell Mai's parents. Someone is on a ladder with coconut leaves, fixing the roof, while Mai's parents supervise below.

Breathless, I gasp: "Can-a-da." Two pairs of raised eyebrows look back at me.

"I'M MOVING TO CANADA!" I shout as Mai and her parents swarm me in a group hug. When they release me from their arms, I explain that I'm leaving tomorrow.

Then I run around the camp and say goodbye to my friends, to Miss Knox, to the priest and to the UNHCR staff and volunteers. I even say farewell to all the buildings that have been home for the past year. I run to the beach to collect a few shells as mementos. My face hurts by evening from a day full of smiling.

As I lie on the mat that night, my mind races, trying to remember everything Vũ told me about Canada. I imagine a cold country full of smiling people. My stomach is tied in happy and nervous knots.

The next morning, I wake up early and slip down to the beach to watch the sunrise. The beautiful orange ball rising into the light blue sky begins the new day. This same sun will be with me on my journey. I wade into the water one last time and try to paint a vivid picture of the beach in my memory. Someday, when I think of living at this camp, I want to remember this beach.

I return to the hut, where Mai's mother has breakfast waiting for me. Then I stuff my few items in a plastic bag. It doesn't take me long to pack.

After one last look around the hut, I grab my bag and

exit for the last time. Mai and I skip along the roadway, with her parents trailing behind, to the bus parked outside the entrance gates of the camp. As I stand in front of the bus, my heart feels like it's skipping, too.

Now that it is time to say a final goodbye, I am not sure what to say. I wish I knew when I will see Mai and her parents again. Outside the bus's door, I twist the handle of my well-used plastic bag containing all that I own. Mai and her parents huddle around me.

"We're going to miss you, Thọ, but I am so happy that you have a new home and will be living with your brother," Mai's mother says.

"We may have an opportunity to move to Australia," says Mai's father, "and once we are settled, maybe you and Vũ can come and visit us."

I look down at the ground. If I look at their faces, I might start to cry, and I'm not sure I'll be able to stop. "I'd like that," I respond.

"See you later, Thọ. I refuse to say goodbye because I know we'll see each other again. Besides, I can't seem to get rid of you. You keep following me everywhere." I raise my eyes and stare at Mai. She smiles her dazzling smile, though I also see tears in her eyes. I secretly paint a picture of her in my mind.

"See you later, too."

Mai has become as close as a sister to me this past year. As we part, Mai wipes her hand against her face, smearing the tears.

I board the bus. Mai's tears are going to make me

cry, too. I am eager to leave Palawan, but it seems every step of my journey brings goodbyes. I sit near the back, and wave out the window to Mai and her parents until they are no longer in sight. I hope that I will see them again someday.

From the bus, I go to the small airport near the camp. I follow the others on the same flight. We walk across the tarmac and climb a set of narrow steps. Then I walk down the aisle to my assigned seat. This is my first plane ride. I am sitting next to a man from the camp. Before the plane takes off, he hands me a piece of gum and explains, "Start chewing this when the plane accelerates. It will prevent popping in your ears from the air pressure."

"Thank you," I respond, not sure what he is talking about.

As the plane's engine begins to roar, I unwrap the piece of gum, put it in my mouth and start chewing. A burst of flavor sweetens my mouth. I grip my hands on the arm rests as the small plane starts to climb higher and higher. For the whole flight, I stare at the back of the seat in front of me and chew and chew and chew. When we get off the plane in Manila, we walk down some steps from the plane onto the tarmac. Then we are escorted to the airport. Although it's definitely bigger than the one in Palawan, the airport isn't crowded. But it's busy enough that I make sure I keep up with the rest of the group. I don't want to lose them.

From the airport, our group is taken by bus to a small intern camp where we will remain for a week while our paperwork and trip get arranged. I want the week to speed by like the jumping snails at Palawan, but each day moves slowly like the gentle seahorses. There isn't much to do at the camp in Manila. It doesn't have a beach or a school.

The only time that I leave the camp is when a group of us ride in a small colorful bus to the main part of town to go shopping. In an earlier letter, Vũ had mailed me an American twenty-dollar bill. I bring it with me on the shopping trip. We wander through covered walkways from one store to the next. Each store has a large window display in the front. With Vũ's money, I buy a duffle bag, a pair of pants and a T-shirt. I also buy two things I've never ever owned: shoes and socks. My whole life I've only worn sandals or flip-flops, but mostly I go barefoot. When I go into another store to purchase an apple, I decide to spend the last of my money on a pack of gum. As soon as I get back to the camp, I hurriedly wash the apple before sinking my teeth into the sweet and crunchy treat, savoring it to the last bite.

***

Finally, the long, boring week has ended! I am sitting in a waiting area in the Manila airport with two other families from the intern camp who are also traveling to Canada. I yawn. I didn't sleep well the night before. Sitting on the floor by my feet is my new bag. It's the only luggage I'm traveling with and contains everything I own. Its contents fit in my hands.

"We're going to live in Montreal," Lan, a teenage girl from one of the families, tells me.

"I'm going to live with my brother near Toronto," I explain. I have no idea where Montreal is or how close it is to where I'll be.

"I'm not looking forward to the flight. My ears popped the whole way when we flew to Manila."

I pull out the package of gum from my pocket and give a silver-wrapped piece to Lan. "Chew this before the plane takes off. It will help stop your ears from popping."

"Thanks, Thọ," Lan says, stuffing the piece in her pocket.

"I wonder how long it will take to get to Toronto? Do you think it will be more than a few hours?"

"I have no idea."

Eventually, it's time to board the plane. It's much bigger than the one I flew on to Manila. I swing my bag as I walk up the steps. A friendly flight attendant helps me find my seat and puts my bag in the compartment above my head. Then I'm left alone. No one around me speaks Vietnamese. Lan and the other refugees are seated elsewhere. I have no one to talk to near me while we're in the air.

Before we take off, I pop a piece of gum in my mouth.

Like with my first flight, I grip the arm rests when the plane charges down the runway. But this time I steal a glance out the window. The buildings and fields whip by at astonishing speed. I do not look out the window again. As the plane's wheels leave earth and soar into the air, my stomach sinks suddenly. I can't believe this huge, heavy machine can fly.

I remember that I survived the sea. I know I will survive the air.

The long flight lands in Tokyo. I didn't see the city from above and will not see it on land, as the other two families and I weave through the bustling crowd to our next plane. The airport is much bigger than the one in Palawan and Manila combined.

During the second flight, a movie plays from a TV hanging from the ceiling in the aisle. Even though I've been learning English, I don't know enough to understand, so I don't bother trying to watch it. A few times, the flight attendants push a cart up the aisle with drinks and food. I recognize the Mountain Dew that Mai's mother gave us during the last lunch with Việt and I point to it on the cart. The flight attendant smiles as she pours some for me into a cup. After I eat and finish the fizzy drink, I walk up and down the aisle to stretch my legs.

I am in the air so long that I watch the sun drop from the sky, hiding from the stars. Then I watch it rise from the clouds, greeting a new day. Sometimes I doze, but I never sleep for long.

Peering out at the fields of white clouds beneath us, lots of questions race through my mind. *What will Canada be like? Will there be snow when I arrive? What will the trees look like? Will there be a beach like at Palawan? Will I recognize Vũ? What will Bryan be like? What does his house look like? Will I get along with the other kids? Will I make friends like Lâm and Việt?*

Even though Vũ told me that I wouldn't see snow in June, I wasn't convinced, especially since so many people have warned me about Canada's cold climate. As the plane circles Toronto, I am amazed at how big it is, with thousands of cars crisscrossing the city like nothing I have ever seen before.

When the plane hits the runway, I dig my nails into my palms to make sure this moment is real. I think back over a year ago when I said goodbye to my parents. The brief hug from my father before my mother and I took the xe lam to the bus station. The trip to my aunt's. Phát driving the small boat along the river to the bigger boat. Looking back at my mother for the last time before Phát guided me to the crowded boat, where I endured pirate attacks daily. Stowing away on two pirate boats. *Cap Anamur*. Almost a year at the refugee camp in Palawan. My first flight from Palawan to Manila. The week at the camp in Manila. Then the flight to Tokyo, and now I am landing in Toronto. After thousands of kilometers, my journey from Vietnam is almost over. I picture the faces of everyone I met along the way as the plane crawls to the gate.

My bag in hand, I am escorted by a flight attendant off the plane. Since she doesn't speak Vietnamese, she waves for me and the other Vietnamese families from the camp to follow her, so we do. She guides us through the sleek terminal.

The airport is massive and clean. It's even bigger than the airports in Tokyo and Manila. We follow the flight attendant down the long, spotless corridor with no garbage littering the shiny ground. We walk through the airport until we arrive at a moving staircase. I am hesitant to put my foot on the first step. The steps look like teeth ready to chew my foot if I slip.

The flight attendant turns around after realizing I'm not beside her and the other Vietnamese families on the moving staircase. She chuckles. Then she motions for me to put one hand on the moving railing as I walk onto a moving step. My legs wobble for a second. Nearing the bottom of the staircase, I discover that the last step disappears into the floor. Before we near the bottom, the flight attendant points to the people on the stairs in front of us to show me how they get off. I take a deep breath and a wider stride, relieved to be off that weird contraption. Walking away, I turn around and watch other people getting on and off without even looking down at their feet. I wonder how long it will take me to get used to moving staircases.

We walk down another hallway to a set of sliding doors. A crowd of people waiting for family and friends hovers on the other side of the doors. After I say good-bye to Lan and her family as well as the other family that flew with me, they disappear into the crowd.

I look around at the sea of unfamiliar faces. *How am I ever going to find Vũ among all these people?* Suddenly I hear a voice calling my name. A voice I haven't heard in a long time. My heart skips. I follow the voice to the edge of the crowd. There he is. Vũ. Next to my brother is a man as tall as a tower with wavy brown hair. He looks like the American and European volunteers at Palawan.

I run toward Vũ. I drop my bag to the floor, wrap my arms around my brother's waist and hug him for the second time in my life. My brother stiffens. Then he hugs me back. Happily, in my brother's arms, I think, *There are so many things I want to tell Vũ. So many stories. So much news.* Instead of sharing all of these thoughts, I pull away from my brother, look up at him and simply say, "You're taller."

Vũ looks down at me and laughs. "You're skinnier."

I grin. We will have lots of time in the days ahead to catch up and talk.

The man reaches out his hand and says in Vietnam-ese, "Welcome to Canada, Thọ." I pull back from Vũ and shake the man's hand.

Vũ says, "Thọ, I want you to meet Bryan."

I smile at the man who has sponsored me to come to Canada.

Bryan smiles back. "Welcome to your new home."

Home.

At last.

***

That night I sleep on the top bunk of a bunk bed in Bryan's bungalow, while Vũ sleeps on the bottom bunk. I hear him tossing and turning, and I smile. I really am back with Vũ. I think of how far away from home we are. I wonder if my parents and sisters will ever join us.

When I finally drift to sleep, I dream that I am back at home in Vietnam. In my dream, I have just carried my cardboard box full of my champion crickets over to Lâm's house.

Lâm meets me at the door. In his hands, he holds his own box, which contains his most winning cricket. Lâm puts his box on the floor.

I take my time picking a cricket. I choose one that isn't the biggest, but I know it's strong. I place it into the box next to Lâm's. The two of us stare intently at our two insects, each hoping ours will win the war.

But the crickets do something completely unexpected and unusual. They don't fight. Nor do they make their angry, chirping noises when priming for battle.

Instead, they stand facing each other, singing cheerfully, and they dance.

Afterword

The Cricket War is based on the journey of Thọ Phạm. Like the boy in the story, twelve-year-old Thọ was obsessed with cricket fighting and soccer. But Thọ's life changed abruptly when his parents arranged for him to escape from Vietnam in 1981 without any family members.

Before leaving Vietnam, Thọ and his mother traveled to an aunt's village, a long bus ride away. There, his mother gave her son a small plastic bag with a change of clothes and some food. She sewed a gold chain into his clothes and wrote her brother's address on the inside of a T-shirt. A week later, a cousin took them in the middle of the night via a tiny boat to another crowded, decrepit boat that Thọ boarded without getting a chance to hug his mother goodbye.

During his seven days on this boat, pirates raided them daily and, once, the boat was attacked twice in one day. The pirates also included fishermen who behaved like pirates, and their attacks, which sometimes vicious, were typical for many of the Vietnamese boats crossing the South China Sea at this time.

During these attacks, the occupants were stripped of

everything valuable, including their food, fresh water and the boat's motors. Believing the unseaworthy vessel he was on would never make land, Thọ hid on a pirates' boat during one of these numerous raids.

These pirates also worked as fishermen, and they treated Thọ well. After a week, they sent him safely onto a second fishing boat, which eventually took him to *Cap Anamur*, as is described in the story.

Cap Anamur is an actual German ship that rescued Vietnamese boats and took the refugees to Palawan. This ship set sail to pick up Vietnamese Boat People in February 1980 and was supported financially by some West Germans led by Dr. Rupert Neudeck. The Germans were inspired by a French group, which sent a ship called *Île de Lumière* to the South China Sea in 1979 to rescue Vietnamese refugees. The French ship only rescued 900 Vietnamese refugees before the program was stopped, as the French government was not prepared to resettle the refugees picked up by *Île de Lumière*.

Cap Anamur, under the leadership of Captain Harry Voss and later Captain Rolf "Papa" Wangnicks, rescued thousands of Vietnamese Boat People traveling across the South China Sea until 1986. Papa (who was the captain when Thọ was aboard) died in 2003, but Huấn, the Vietnamese translator mentioned in the story, lives in Germany today.

Under the guidance of Bernd Göken, *Cap Anamur* continues to operate today, providing humanitarian aid in countries such as Afghanistan, Somalia and Sierra

Leone. The German not-for-profit organization no longer operates via the ship *Cap Anamur*, though it still uses the ship's name as the name of its organization.

Việt, the friend Thọ met on *Cap Anamur*, is based on a real person. This friend did get flown to Singapore for emergency surgery. The real Việt didn't travel with his mother but with his uncle and uncle's family. All of them spent time living in Palawan before moving to California, where Việt lives today. Thọ has visited him three times since their incredible journey.

From *Cap Anamur*, Thọ lived at the refugee camp in Palawan for six months. Palawan was one of many United Nations Refugee Agency camps where Vietnamese refugees lived for a few months or even years while waiting to get into one of many countries accepting refugees. Here volunteer teachers, such as Muriel Knox (Thọ's favorite teacher), taught the refugees English and tried to prepare them for the Western world. Though many refugee camps continue to operate around the world today, Palawan closed its doors in 1996.

After Palawan, Thọ spent the next six months at an intern camp in Manila. He eventually traveled to Canada on a flight with Lan and her family. Thọ was sponsored by Bryan, a schoolteacher from Richmond Hill, a suburb of Toronto. Bryan adopted seven Vietnamese youth in the 1980s, including Thọ, all of whom had left their parents behind in Vietnam as they escaped the Communist regime. Today, Bryan is a proud grandfather and great-grandfather.

Four years after his arrival, Thọ became a Canadian citizen. In 1996 he graduated from Ryerson University (now known as Toronto Metropolitan University) in Toronto as an electrical engineer. He currently lives and works in a small Canadian city with his wife and two children. Thọ's father actually left Vietnam before his son, but his mother remained behind. It wasn't until 1991 that Thọ traveled back to Vietnam and saw his mother for the first time since leaving ten years earlier.

Although the framework of this story is based on Thọ's journey, it could not have been told without the help of Thọ's adopted brother, Độ, and his wife, Nghĩa. They also shared the story of their remarkable journey to Canada with me. Athough Nghĩa did not travel with Thọ and she ended up at a different refugee camp, a number of the details in the story and the descriptions are based on Nghĩa's incredible journey.

The character of Vũ is fictional. While Thọ does have two brothers, his parents could not afford for all three sons to leave Vietnam, so the other brothers were left at home, where the eldest of the two was conscripted into the army.

Lâm's family is also fictional, though Lâm and his brother's disappearance is authentic. Some historians believe as many as half the Boat People fleeing Vietnam drowned at sea. Though Mai is also fictional, she is a composite of a number of young Vietnamese girls.

Unlike in the story, Thọ did not meet up with the people from his original boat at Palawan. He did learn later, however, that his boat arrived safely in Thailand a week after he had escaped on the pirate boat. Ironically, if Thọ had stayed on his boat, he would have made it to a refugee camp much earlier.

The incidents in this story, from the descriptions of the pirate raids to the mother who thought her baby had died after she fed him cough syrup to keep him quiet happened, either to Thọ or one of the Boat People I interviewed. Even though Minh and Quỳnh are also fictional, they represent real thugs who bullied the other Vietnamese at the various refugee camps. The big fight, caused by Minh and Quỳnh, was inspired by a three-day war that occurred at Nghĩa's refugee camp.

The world wasn't initially kind to the Vietnamese refugees, but various countries around the world accepted them, with the United States taking the majority, more than a million people. From 1975 to 1991, Canada accepted 141 113 Vietnamese Boat People. Today, many of these refugees are Canadian citizens and have built their lives, and their children's lives, in Canada.

— Sandra McTavish

A Brief Recent History of Vietnam

Before Thọ was born, Vietnam was a colony of France. The French left Vietnam in 1954, and the country was divided into two political regions. A Communist government led North Vietnam, while a democratic government led South Vietnam.

Following this division, a civil war broke out between North Vietnam and South Vietnam. Many Vietnamese, including Thọ's parents, did not want to live under Communist rule, especially because, as Catholics, they weren't able to practice their religion freely.

Eventually the United States sent troops to Vietnam to try to stop the spread of Communism. They came in the early 1960s and stayed until the mid-1970s. A war — known as the Vietnam War — ravaged the country.

The United States government pulled out its troops following the Paris Peace Accord, which was signed in 1973. This accord was intended to stop the fighting between North and South Vietnam, though peace didn't last for very long. On April 30, 1975, the Communists took over the South Vietnamese capital city, changing its name from Sài Gòn to Hồ Chí Minh City after their leader.

After the reunification, the Communist government made life miserable for the former supporters of the

South Vietnamese government. Over a million people were sent to camps, imprisoned or tortured simply because they had ties to the former government. Men and boys from South Vietnam also worried about being forced into the army. The fear of the Communists, along with incredible poverty and the inability to practice their religion freely, inspired hundreds of thousands of Vietnamese, mostly from South Vietnam, to escape on tiny, homemade boats.

These boats of Vietnamese refugees dotted the South China Sea from 1975 until the mid-1990s. Many of the people on these boats had no idea where they were heading. They just knew they didn't want to live in a Communist country. Most hoped to end up in America, the country that had tried saving them during the war. However, even some of the most educated Vietnamese had no realistic idea of how far away America was.

The trip on the sea was treacherous, and many died. The lucky ones ended up in refugee camps in countries such as Thailand, the Philippines and Malaysia. They often lived there in poverty for months, even years, until they were accepted into another country.

These people were known as the Boat People. While news reports spoke of them, few people in the rest of the world really knew the horrific details of their journey. Even today many Vietnamese won't speak about their trip from their homeland.

A Communist government continues to lead Vietnam, one of the few remaining Communist countries in the world today.

Thọ's Acknowledgments

Thank you to Sandra for her unwavering commitment and Kids Can Press for its wonderful support to make this book possible. Without Sandra's dedication, this story would be forgotten, like the plight of hundreds of thousands of Vietnamese Boat People who escaped Vietnam during the two decades following the fall of Sài Gòn in 1975. I am so grateful that this story is getting told while countless other more worthy and deserving stories forever remain untold in people's hearts.

Along my voyage to freedom, I owe my debt of gratitude to Captain Wangnicks and the crew of *Cap Anamur* and everyone supporting their great cause. You were God's angels watching over us in our times of need in the treacherous ocean. To Ms. Muriel Knox, other teachers, priests, doctors, nurses, UNHCR and government officials, volunteers, local residents and all others who selflessly donated their time and efforts to help the boat people in all aspects of our journey, your compassion and kindness became our ray of hope while we were in the camps awaiting resettlement. It was my privilege and honor to have known many of you, and I have made lifelong friends during my journey.

Thank you from the bottom of my heart to Canada and its people, my adoptive father, Bryan, his family, St. Matthew's United Church and everyone else who gave us a second chance in life. We have been blessed to call Canada home, and we feel that it is the greatest country on Earth because of its gentle, caring and compassionate people. My father is a shining example; he has dedicated his life to helping us and many others ever since he became aware of the refugee crisis in the late 1970s. His unconditional love has been guiding us for over four decades, and we cannot ever imagine what our lives would have been without him.

As a final note, my life would not be rewarding without the love and support of my wife and children, and for that, I truly love them with all my heart.

Sandra's Acknowledgments

It takes a village to publish a novel. With that in mind, I have many people to thank.

Truly, I am indebted to my friend Thọ. Without him, there would be no novel. I thank Thọ for sharing all that he could remember of a story that I suspect wasn't easy to tell. I truly appreciate the countless hours he spent talking to me, reading and adding his comments and corrections to multiple drafts, and answering my many, many questions. Thanks also to Thọ's wife and their sons for the times our conversations and this novel took him away from them.

This novel would still be tucked away in a folder on my computer if it wasn't for the great people at Kids Can Press. A special thanks to Lara Caplan and Yasemin Uçar for getting this novel the green light, and Patricia Ocampo for patiently coaching a pair of novice authors. Without a doubt, Patricia's detailed edits and thoughtful suggestions made our words shine. Other shoutouts go to Patti Tasko, Catherine Dorton, Tenzin Tsering and Marie Bartholomew, designer.

Thanks to Thọ's father for meeting with me on several occasions, telling me the story of how his seven kids came to Canada, and, most importantly, for being a very close friend to the McTavish clan.

Thanks also to Thọ's adopted brother, Độ, and his wife, Nghĩa, along with their delightful children, Bryan and Stephanie, who were children when I started this project and are now wonderful young adults. I have enjoyed numerous delicious Vietnamese meals at Độ and Nghĩa's home and appreciate the many hours they spent sharing with me their stories as Boat People.

I also want to express my gratitude to the other Vietnamese refugees who shared their stories with me: Thọ's adopted sister Vân, along with Minh Phan, Salt (Phạm) Thị Trường, Lễ Trần, Phương Chi Trần, Bảo Vũ, Hùng Vũ and Linh Vũ. Vân also provided me with a written account of her journey to Canada that she wrote as a high school assignment a few years after arriving.

I am grateful to Julie Wetzler, whose pictures of Vietnam helped me visualize the place, and to Rivka Cranley, who has always encouraged me as a writer and once gave me a wonderful piece of advice that prompted me to begin researching this novel: Write a story that has yet to be told. I am indebted to Jack Martindale, Kevin Martindale, Jennifer McClorey, Ann Featherstone and Mary Beth Leatherdale for their insights on how to improve my manuscript, as well as my friend Donna Guerra for her encouragement and support.

A special thanks goes to Norman Aisbett, a retired journalist from Australia who spent five weeks aboard *Cap Anamur* in 1981 and visited the refugee camp in Palawan. Norman kindly mailed me his articles written during this time and answered my inquisitive emails.

I also appreciate the emails answering my questions about *Cap Anamur* from its current managing director, Bernd Göken.

Aside from factual articles, I am surprised by how few Boat People have shared their stories publicly. Though I read what I could find in the library, one book in particular was invaluable: *The Boat People: An 'Age' Investigation* by Bruce Grant (Penguin Books, 1980). I also found the film *Journey from the Fall* by Hàm Trần helpful.

Finally, I would be lost without the love and support of my inner circle: Linda Krepinsky, Avalon Martin-McTavish, Ian McTavish, Liam McTavish, Marni Martin-McTavish, Miesha McTavish, C.J. Ringled and Todd McTavish. A special shoutout goes to my parents, John and Marion McTavish, who read and edited numerous drafts and have always encouraged me; and my wonderful partner, Doug Reid.